STORIES FOR BIRDERS AND OTHER OBSERVERS

Andrea Vojtko

WingSpan Press

Published in the United States and the United Kingdom by WingSpan Press, Livermore, CA

The WingSpan name, logo and colophon are the trademarks of WingSpan Publishing.

ISBN 978-1-59594-574-7 (pbk.)
ISBN 978-1-59594-906-6 (ebk.)

First edition 2015

Printed in the United States of America

www.wingspanpress.com

Library of Congress Control Number 2015956861

1 2 3 4 5 6 7 8 9 10

FOR MY PARENTS

CONTENTS

Foreword

Famed *New Yorker* short story editor and master of the form himself, William Maxwell writes in his essay collection *The Outermost Dream*: "I can never get enough of knowing about other people's lives." Andrea Vojtko's short story collection is a magnificent representation of that sentiment – how we are wired to be curious about other people. It's fair to invoke Maxwell since Vojtko's stories are carefully crafted in terms of conflict, pacing, character, idiom, and ending. Moreover, Vojtko goes further and demonstrates the inquisitive human tendency to explore our place in the natural world. Specifically, Vojtko manages in many stories to weave a connection between the complex relationships among people and the human interaction with nature. Readers open a window to see how the natural world and especially birds, whether flocking vultures or a solitary heron, intersect in and impact the lives of people (as in "Swirling Above Her Head" and "The All-Knowing Eye"). Vojtko's stories explore with humor and poignancy the peculiar behavior constituent of the human condition without forcing answers on readers. We don't have any real heroes here; we have idiosyncratic and highly sympathetic characters who reflect human nature with their foibles, quirks, broken lives, and ultimately a quest for meaning (as in "Searching for Life on Mars," "A Year in Beverly Hills," "Of Persimmons and Asian Pears," and "Marvelous"). Reading a Vojtko story is a special experience, where one enters a wondrous and even at times bizarre world, her writing reminiscent of another short story master, Flannery O'Connor. There is a fine line dividing reality and fantasy, and these stories are filled with magical drama and dark comedy though quite believable. There are situations where some odd circumstance gets compounded by chance incrementally and builds to a strange outcome (as in "Chasing the Loon"). The essence of a character is crystallized quickly in dialogue and actions, where, for instance Vojtko wonderfully captures the difference between men and women or the paradoxical ties between parent and child (as in "I Stop for Falcons," "Jubilant Voices," and "Meditating Like Brutus"). In real life we often don't get to know someone deeply, but in the space of a Vojtko story we come to know the inner thoughts, pains, and sufferings of individuals and how their lives converge meaningfully with other people (as in "Stations of the Cross").

Andrea Vojtko's collection of literary stories populated with memorable characters, resounding with crisp idioms, and flavored with the sounds, textures, and colors of nature in the Mid-Atlantic States is highly recommended for anyone curious about the lives of other people.

Gregory F. Tague, Ph.D.
Professor of English, St. Francis College, N.Y.
General Editor, Bibliotekos

Preface

Birders are among the keenest observers and five of the thirteen short stories in this collection are inspired by imagination while birding or connecting with nature. Ida Pilcher is inexplicably followed wherever she goes by a dozen turkey vultures; Garland Duckett sees God in the golden eye of a Great Blue Heron; Nelson Mayfield, driven by an Internet report, searches frantically for life on Mars before his anticipated early demise. I find incongruences in human behavior to be humorous and I am fascinated by the idea that many people are consumed by an esoteric interest or activity. Nathanael Early's dioramas of Civil War battlefields have taken over his basement; he barely has space for Vicksburg; Brian Feeney observes his neighbor, an Iraq war veteran, refurbishing a corroded four-foot bronze cross on his deck. I believe that even "normal" people are eccentric in their own way, if you observe them long enough.

Because I have spent so much of my leisure time on field trips in forests, marshes, seashores, bogs, mountains, and canal paths, ideas for short stories occurred to me in natural settings. Often I was inspired by just one curious thought about my surroundings which I then developed into a story purely from my imagination. I don't subscribe to the short story model that everything has an answer and must be explained in studious detail. I believe we can observe nature like a scientist and report on our conclusions but that there will always be some mystery in nature. In other words we will be more at peace if we search for answers as best we can and honor this process by accepting our findings and the uncertainty that remains. While engaged in searching we have to guard against not seeing the forest for the trees.

The two short story writers that I have benefited from the most are Flannery O'Connor and Frank O'Connor (not related to Flannery.) Although their writing is dissimilar, they share some common theories about the art of the short story and the art of fiction. In his book, *The Lonely Voice: A Study of the Short Story* Frank O'Connor suggests that the novel is about "normal" society. He believes the short story is about characters on the fringes of society: the lonely idealist, the artist, dreamers, spoiled priests, and people who don't quite fit in. The short story has no hero. I subscribe to Frank O'Connor's short story theories as described in *The Lonely Voice*.

Flannery O'Connor has written the purest kind of short stories where not one word more or less is needed; her stories are perfectly distilled. Her characters are vivid, stark, grotesque, generally unlikable but always fascinating; you cannot look away. She believed that stories defy analysis, that what she is saying in the story cannot be said any other way and it takes every word in the story to say what the meaning is. I have reread her stories repeatedly since my college days and am sure they have a significant impact on my writing. Notes on my previously published short stories are contained in the back of the book.

I appreciate the sound advice I received in The Writer's Center workshops in Bethesda, Maryland that I attended over the years especially from the following instructors: Susan Land, Kate Blackwell, Ann McLaughlin, Ellen Herbert, and Brenda Clough. I am also grateful to the naturalists in the Audubon Naturalist Society in Chevy Chase, Maryland for all of the wonderful field trips they've provided; I'm especially thankful to naturalists Stephanie Mason and Mark Garland.

I am grateful for the support that Gregory F. Tague, Literature Professor at St. Francis College in Brooklyn, New York, has provided me in previously publishing my work and for his suggestion and encouragement to publish a separate collection of my short stories. Gregory Tague is also the Editor of several literary Anthologies published by Editions Bibliotekos and the author of *Making Mind: Moral Sense and Consciousness in Philosophy, Science and Literature* and *Art and Adaptation.* I would also like to thank Fredericka Jacks, Editions Bibliotekos publisher, for her support.

Andrea Vojtko

Swirling Above Her Head

Ida Pilcher was peering through the storefront window of Lou's TV Repair shop anxious about the vulture she spotted high in the sky. Blinded by the late September sun, she looked down and caught her reflected image in the grimy plate glass causing her to frown. Her middle-aged face was puffy and was beginning to take the shape of a potato, as was her short squat body.

Floyd Beasley pulled his van into Lou's parking lot in front of the store and Ida went over to the shelf against the far wall to get his still-broken nine-year old TV. With an audible grunt, she hoisted the 25-inch set onto the counter.

"Did you fix it?" Floyd asked entering the shop.

"Look here, Floyd, your cats peed in this TV and they shorted the connections," she said elevating her monotone voice. "Our warranty doesn't cover cat pee. See. It says right here." She pointed to a clause in fine print.

"What are you talking about? You better not give me a lot of rubbish about this warranty," he shouted pushing away the warranty papers she held out to him.

"Floyd, you can leave and take your TV with you. I'm not taking that kind of stuff," Ida said.

"What good's a warranty if you have an excuse for everything?" he ranted. "Good for nothing," he mumbled.

"What did you say?"

"I said you're good for nothing," he said.

"Leave now, Floyd. I don't have to take that."

Floyd picked up his TV, grumbling, and banged the door as he left.

Ida didn't appreciate Floyd saying she was good for nothing. Everybody in Hobbs knew she was a hard worker at Lou's and when she worked at Nelson's Hardware store and when she was a waitress at the Cozy Diner. She couldn't help what the warranty read.

"His cables!" She grabbed them from the counter and rushed outside to catch him before he left. She didn't want to leave the shop because of the vulture problem. It made her nervous. For the past two weeks about a dozen turkey vultures swirled in a vortex fifty feet above her head every time she went outside. Then they followed her or her Chevy 4x4 pickup around town. It was peculiar and she was afraid to mention it to anyone.

As she approached Floyd's van with the cables, she caught sight of several vultures descending in the sky above her.

"What did you bring those buzzards with you for?" he smirked following her gaze upward. She turned and walked back to the shop.

It was time to close the store, but she waited another half hour hoping the vultures would fly away. Finally she put on her bulky West Virginia Mountaineers jacket to leave, opened the door slowly, and made a break for the battered Chevy truck she parked across the lot. Like evil omens, ten or twelve vultures swooped over the roof from behind the shop and caught up with her as she got to her truck. They were about as high as the four-story building next door and their scary six-foot wingspan was tilted slightly upward in a "V-shape." Their bald red turkey heads looked down at her making her feel nauseous as they spiraled above her head, descending and rising, descending and rising.

What the dang was happening? Vultures go after road-kill and dead things. She wondered if they smelled something in her and imagined a large decaying growth within her body. Stop thinking about silly things, she told herself. As she headed home, she turned to look at an outside mirror she had tilted upward on the back of her truck and saw the vultures still following her.

Looking at her watch, she thought about feeding her family. She decided to stop at the Burger Boy to get take-out for supper.

"Four Burger Boy's and four large fries," she said into the microphone at the drive-through.

"Do you want the meal?" a foreign voice asked.

"No. No soda," she answered. She wasn't paying for extras.

At the pickup window a middle-aged Indian woman with a red dot on her forehead and a broad smile handed her a bag of burgers and fries. Ida noticed her nameplate read, "Shanti." She gave her a twenty and waited for her change. After a long minute, Shanti handed her the change and in a sing-song tone chimed, "Have a beautiful evening." Ida was too busy counting the coins to respond. Once she was short-changed by a foreigner working at the Burger Boy and she wasn't going to let that happen again.

Ida twisted back to look into her tilted mirror and noticed the vultures were still there. When she turned forward, Shanti was leaning out the window watching her. Ida's husband, Duane, and her two boys, Ernie and Frankie, were the only ones who knew about the vultures before Floyd saw them. Now this Indian lady knows, she thought.

When Ida got to her farmhouse two miles outside town, she left the burgers, fries and a pitcher of lemonade on the kitchen table and told her sons to dig in. She took a few beers and burghers and went over to Duane's hubcap shop next to the house. The shop was a two-story white cinderblock building similar to a small warehouse. The lower floor had a wall-sized window decorated with a variety of hubcaps arranged around the edge. Every ornate and modern variation of swirling chrome spokes and sculpted air holes decorated the hubcaps. Some had four or five thick lug nuts in the center; others had smooth centers either flattened like a Frisbee or elevated like a dome. From the road they gave the impression of elaborately-designed silver buttons. Stenciled in the middle of the window in faded red letters were the words "Hubcap Heaven."

"I got take-out today, Duane; I was running late," she said as she lumbered into the store. Shelves and crates of old hubcaps, both sparkling and grimy, overwhelmed the interior.

"How come you're running late?" Duane's attention was riveted on the spokes of a hubcap he was polishing. He was six feet, lanky, and still good-looking with his little moustache and wavy black hair.

"Them vultures are still following me around," Ida answered.

"Yeh? It's the weirdest thing," he said stopping his work to plunge into the burgers and beer Ida dropped on the counter. She sat on a stool and joined him.

"They have it out for you for some reason, Ida," Duane said.

"What did I do?" Ida asked.

"Not a damn thing," he answered engrossed in his meal. He and Ida got married when they were both twenty-two and Ida discovered she was pregnant. At first Duane worked in the coal mines but he squirreled away enough money to build the hubcap shop he had dreamed about.

"Well, then why are they after me?" The vultures suggested scary things, a freak of nature or something weird or supernatural. Ida didn't know too much about nature even though she'd lived her entire life surrounded by mountains and wildlife in West Virginia. Nor was she religious. Yes, sometimes she took her two boys, Ernie and Frankie, to the Church of the Assembly, but she wanted to teach them about guilt feelings so they didn't think they could do anything they wanted.

"I don't know why they're following you. Anything unusual happen at Lou's lately?" Duane mumbled chewing his food.

"No, the same old things. Floyd Beasley got bent out of shape today when we wouldn't fix his TV. He started sassing me," she said. "But you know me, Duane, I told him to take his business someplace else if he was going to cuss at me. I had to take the cables out to his van and them vultures were right there and he saw them and made fun of me."

"You want me to go and bust his chops?" Duane asked playfully jabbing her arm.

"No. You'll make matters worse," she said. "Them vultures are following me for about two weeks now. They started following me for no reason I can figure."

"Don't worry about it. They'll go away sooner or later," he tried to reassure her.

The next evening Ida decided to make a country supper for her family instead of relying on fast food. She carried a baked ham with pineapple rings, brown sugar and cloves to the table and candied sweet potatoes. Finally she brought over a plate of steaming corn on the cob. The comforting smell of home-cooking filled the farmhouse.

"Frankie, Ernie, supper's ready," she yelled through the opened kitchen window. They were playing catch in front of the hubcap shop.

Duane was sitting at the table reading the classifieds in the evening edition of the Hobbs Gazette looking for hubcap deals. He would travel to car junkyards or shows to get supplies but a lot of people came to him with their old hubcaps and he had a reputation for giving them a fair price for a 60's Ford spinner or a Cadillac wire spoke. If he wasn't around, Ida knew enough to tell a good hubcap from a dud.

Frankie and Ernie came in, slumped into their chairs at the table and reached for the food Ida had prepared. Frankie was eleven; Ernie was a senior in high school.

"Hey, partner," Duane said pushing Ernie playfully in his thin shoulders. "You know, I was thinking, Ida, why don't we send this guy to college next year? Get us a college graduate in the family."

Ida concentrated on slicing her ham and didn't answer immediately. "You know what I think about college, Duane," she said finally, as if the issue was settled a long time ago.

"I want to be a writer or a reporter for CNN," Ernie said enthusiastically.

Ida looked at Ernie, "A writer? What kind of money are you going to make being a writer? You think CNN is going to have a reporter in West Virginia?"

Ida chewed her food looking off in the distance. "What you want to do is get a job on the new bypass highway, driving heavy equipment. There's where the money is. You can count on heavy equipment to give you a good living."

"Ernie's not big enough for construction, Ida. Look at him," Duane said. Ida looked at her puny offspring. He didn't take after her side. "He can grow yet," she said unconvincingly.

"I'll work on the bypass, Mom," little Frankie said, "I'll learn how to drive heavy equipment."

"Good, Frankie. Eat your ham so you get big and strong," Ida said.

"If you go to college you can do a lot of things," Duane said.

"You name one kid in West Virginia who went to college and got a good job here," Ida said.

"George Boone went to college and he's the editor of the Gazette," Duane said shuffling the paper.

Ida took a section of the Hobbs Gazette from Duane and

said, "Look at this stuff: 'County to Spray for Mosquitos.'"
She opened to the next page, "'Rob Taylor to run for Sheriff.'
Now how's he going to be sheriff when he's even afraid to go
hunting?" She turned the page to the Obituaries. Her mouth
dropped open. "What? What is this? 'Ida Pilcher Dead at 40.'
It's here under the obituaries, Duane."

Duane took the paper from her. "What's going on? Who
printed that?" He read the whole obituary in a slow, confused
tone, "Ida Pilcher, longtime resident of Hobbs, died unexpect-
edly of cardiac arrest at age 40..." Duane concluded the article
"... She is survived by her husband, Duane, and sons, Ernest
and Frank."

"It's a mistake," he said, "I'll call the newspaper."

"What kind of joke is this?" Ida said. "Is this dead?" She
stood and held her arms out wide so everyone there could witness her fully functioning body.

"I'll call the Gazette." Duane got up.

"No, let me call," Ida said. "I bet this is Randy Beasley,
Floyd's brother. He works there. This is crazy." She and Duane
went into the living room and she dialed the Gazette but the
office was closed so she found George Boone's number to call
him at his house. Duane went to answer a knock on the kitchen
door. Ida could see old Mrs. Lowery, who volunteered at the
Church of the Assembly, standing in the kitchen with a casserole dish, her eyes red and puffy. "I'm so sorry," she said to
Duane, "Your poor boys."

"It's a mistake, Mrs. Lowery," Duane said, "It's a bad mistake." Mrs. Lowery who was hard of hearing continued to cry.
She put the casserole with the other food and threw her arms
around Ernie and Frankie. Duane turned to the living room toward Ida who was yelling on the phone, "What's wrong with
you at your newspaper? Don't you check your facts? I can't
believe you could be so ignorant." There was a pause for a few

brief seconds but then she continued, "Don't give me that. I know Randy Beasley's done this. I'm not going to take this. You'll see."

Mrs. Lowery, still tearful in the kitchen, was trying to comfort the boys who continued to eat their dinner. Duane was pacing from the kitchen to the living room and back again. Little Frankie took a spoonful of the macaroni and cheese casserole Mrs. Lowery had brought.

Ida slammed the phone and went back to the kitchen, her face as red as her baked ham. Mrs. Lowery put her hand to her mouth and gasped. Ida said, "Could you believe a newspaper could do such a thing?" She threw it on the table. "And you want your son to go into the newspaper business." Mrs. Lowery went over to Duane and Ida and threw her arms around them and began singing, "Amazing Grace." Little Frankie joined in with her. Ernie laughed about the whole thing and Duane and Ida stood there bewildered.

During the evening Ida's phone rang with condolences which she greeted with the caveat that she was planning to remain around for thirty or forty years. Mrs. Keegan from the Farmers Co-op brought over peach cobbler and the Gazette sent over a fruit basket with an apology. Two funeral directors called, one of whom she could not convince she was in fine health. "Please consider Murphy's Funeral Home when the time approaches," he said.

The next morning Ida called Lou. "Yes, I'm still alive but I got me a migraine something awful over the whole thing."

"Take a couple of days off, Ida," Lou said. "You're very appreciated over here. We collected $75 for flowers already. Should I send a check to the American Heart Association like it said in the obituary?"

This threw Ida into a fury. As soon as she hung up she ran outside, got into her truck, and headed over to the Hobbs

Gazette office on Main Street. She hardly even noticed the persistent vultures overhead with their dizzying swirls.

"I want a retraction on the front page with a recent photo so people will stop sending me condolences and I want to know whose idea of a joke this is. I would bet you anything it's that Randy Beasley," she said to George Boone.

"I don't know who put it in there, Ida," George said, "I proofread it but, honest to God, I thought you passed. I was quite sad about the whole thing. I'll get to the bottom of it and I promise I'll put your picture on the front page tonight with a complete retraction and an apology."

He phoned Mickey, the Gazette's photographer, and asked him to take a picture of Ida outside the Gazette building in front of the large digital date display. Ida followed him outside, and after a few snaps, she got in her Chevy truck and headed home to try to calm herself down. She lay on the living room couch with a cold washcloth on her forehead trying to recover from her continuing migraine.

Duane came home about five with the paper in his hand and a look of gloom. "What's wrong, Duane? What's wrong?" He looked down at the paper. She pulled it from his hand to the horror of her picture on the front page with four vultures in view hovering over her head. The headline read, "Ida Pilcher Alive despite Being Pursued by Vultures." The story was by Randy Beasley.

Ida hurried to the Gazette before it closed and marched into George Boone's office. "I want Randy Beasley fired for this story," she said shaking the front page at him. "He's doing this because I wouldn't fix Floyd's TV."

"Well, this is a different twist now, Ida. If you've got a flock of vultures following you, that's real news. I never heard of such a thing. I have to report it or else I'm not doing my job. There's a lot of public interest in this story I'm

9

finding out. I got a lot of calls about it already. And people are concerned buzzards might start increasing in Hobbs. You know, they regurgitate that stuff they eat and it's a real mess. The smell. Whew!"

"Now don't make it worse than it is. They never regurgitated anything and they've been hanging around my place for two weeks." She was sorry as soon as the words came out but continued, "I want the story retracted tomorrow or I'm going to get Attorney Carney to sue your paper."

"I can't retract what's real news. Besides the Associated Press has already picked it up and put it on their wire. We never had that happen to us in Hobbs," he said with pride, "We could have other newspaper reporters out here even."

"Expect to see Attorney Carney," Ida threatened and slammed the door to his office. She walked out of the Gazette and got into her truck with the vultures waiting for her. The lowest ones were right above the maple tree next to her truck, their red turkey heads staring down into her uplifted eyes.

"I'm going to wring your necks," she scowled at them.

When she got home she jumped out of her truck and stood there, legs akimbo, firmly planted on the ground, hands on her hips, looking up at the vultures swirling above her head. You can't win in this world, she thought. How could she control the entire sky? If she could, she'd kill the ugly beasts. She ran into the house and came out with Duane's shotgun, raised the gun toward the sky and began shooting at the buzzards but they dispersed in a wide spiral. She chased after them yelling, "Get down here now, cowards." She kept shooting until she got one. It flopped down with a thud in the vegetable garden. Duane came running out of the shop looking alarmed.

"I shot one of those damn buzzards," she said glancing at him. "It's in the cabbage patch." She marched toward the house.

"You can't shoot birds out of season. You know that," Duane said coming after her.

"That's not a bird. It's the devil from hell." She went into the house and slammed the door.

The next day an unfamiliar car stopped at the farmhouse and a stranger dressed in a tweed jacket and a turtleneck sweater got out. Ida observed him through one of the front windows. When he knocked, she opened the front door and stared at him through the locked screen door.

"Hello, I'm Professor Yates from West Virginia University. I've read about the vultures that are bothering you down here and I thought I might be able to help out."

Ida sized him up and then opened the screen door. "C'mon in," she said showing him into the parlor.

"Could you explain the whole situation?" the professor asked as he relaxed in her cushioned chair next to the fireplace. Ida perched on the sofa and went over every single detail.

"You know, birds can be imprinted with someone who raises them or they see when they are born. Did you inadvertently coddle the birds, perhaps?"

Ida paused and then shrieked, "They're buzzards, for God's sake. Why would I coddle a buzzard?"

"Look, I'm trying to help," the professor said. He started rattling on about different cases where birds were imprinted with humans whom they took to be their parents. Ida stared at him thinking this was a lot of stuff. He didn't know shit from shinola. She rose abruptly, "I gotta get to work. When you think of how I can get rid of these pests, come tell me." She ushered him out of her house.

As his car left, an SUV took his place and five men and women dressed almost entirely in shades of beige with big brimmed hats and binoculars hanging around their necks, jumped out of the car resembling a swat team of park rangers and raised their binoculars to the sky.

Ida marched out to them. "What do you want around here?" she said.

"We're birders. We came to see the vultures," one of them replied.

"You never seen a vulture before? They're all over the state. You don't have to come out here," she said. "This is a business here. If you don't want a hubcap, go someplace else to look for vultures."

"That could be it," one of the birders cried. "Birds are attracted by shiny objects. They could be attracted by the hubcaps in your truck there." Ida looked over at her old Chevy and the pile of gleaming hubcaps thrown in the back.

"Duane has a lot of hubcaps in his truck. Why don't they follow him?"

"I don't know. Birds can be pretty peculiar. There's no accounting for some of their behavior. Once there were starlings that crawled into the coin deposit box at a car wash and carried quarters in their beaks to the flat roof of the building. They found 16,000 quarters on the car wash roof after they installed a video cam and caught the birds right in the act. They may be attracted to the hubcaps because they gleam or maybe they're attracted to a specific type of hubcap."

"So you don't know why they're following me?" Ida said.

"No. Not yet. But maybe something will come to us. We have a lot of bird experience here."

"Yeh, I can see that," she mumbled, opening the door of her truck. "Duane will help you if you want to buy a hubcap."

The vultures followed her over to her truck, their menacing eyes stalking her every move preparing to accompany her to town. One birder captured their departure with his video camera.

When she got to Lou's, the parking lot was filled with cars and reporters from the media.

"There she is," shouted a reporter. Snapping cameras trailed her as she ran into the store past a mob of reporters which were blocking several of Lou's customers from carrying their TV's into the shop. After several days of this circus atmosphere, Ida agreed for the good of Lou's business, she would take an extended vacation without pay.

But since she believed in keeping busy, she decided to help Duane organize his hubcap shop. "It's an H915 Mustang hubcap, Duane. Don't put it there. It belongs on the 6E shelves. They're marked right here." Duane frowned but his business grew since they were getting a lot of visitors who came to see Ida's vultures and Ida made a rule requiring visitors to buy a hubcap if they came within fifty feet of her house.

Every birder, professor, reporter or sightseer who visited lined up to buy a hubcap. The hubcap line stretched clear around the old oak tree on the other side of the house.

Duane took advantage of the increase in sales by hitting the road to get extra hubcaps from the junkyards and car dealers he used. Ida and Ernie worked in the store, and little Frankie had a lemonade stand outside.

But in late October, birders and sightseers began to drop off and Duane became overstocked with hubcaps. The weather was getting gloomy as the seasons began to change and Ida was miserable with nothing much to do and no one to talk to. Half the time Duane and his buddies, Mo and Jake, went on the road trying to unload the excess hubcaps. And no one in Hobbs seemed much interested in visiting with the "Dead Vulture Lady" as people now referred to her. No one wanted to take a chance on having a vulture throw up on them with half-eaten carrion. That was the buzz around Hobbs even though there was not one single incident of the kind.

One morning when Ida stopped for a doughnut at the Tasty Bakery a few of the vultures descended ten feet above her head. Their beaks were open and the sheer size of them intimidated everyone near the Bakery. The entire parking lot cleared in five minutes with people screaming and dropping their doughnuts and coffee. After this, everyone avoided Ida and went the other way when they saw her coming as though she was possessed by demons. Even when she went to the Burger Boy at night for a fruit smoothie she could hardly get anyone to take her order, much less join her for a little conversation.

Only the Indian woman, Shanti, treated her normally. "Fruit Smoothie?" she would ask with her perpetual smile and Ida would say, "Yeh, the regular," and nod at her with a slight grin. Ida began going to the Burger Boy late at night for a fruit smoothie so she could have a pleasant exchange with someone.

One night near closing time Shanti came to the corner booth where Ida was sitting and said, "You look very unhappy."

"I have my troubles," Ida said.

"In India we say accept your troubles and you will be at peace with the world," Shanti said, waving her right palm upward.

"Well, you see, I have these vultures following me everywhere I go. They're out there now," Ida said gesturing toward the parking lot. "What can I do?"

"You can accept them," Shanti said cheerfully, "They are your vultures. They were sent to you."

This sounded like a lot of stuff to Ida but she said, "Maybe so." She slurped the smoothie and then said, "Well, I have to go now. Maybe I'll be here tomorrow."

Her life was miserable, day after day, week after week, with no companionship but her own family and even they had become tight-lipped since their friends weren't coming around much. She never believed in wasting time being sad before but she was slipping into a deep melancholy.

One evening in early November Duane and the boys were watching wrestling. Ida looked at her watch and thought she might be able to make it to the Burger Boy before it closed.

Shanti came over to talk with her after she got her fruit smoothie. "I think it means you are very special."

"I don't want to be special," Ida said but she began going to the Burger Boy nightly to talk to Shanti.

One day in late November, she went outside and gazed upward at the vultures, lifted her hands in the air like a preacher and shouted, "O.K. I accept you vultures. I accept you as my own."

Duane came rushing out of the shop, "What happened?"

"Nothing, Duane." She continued to look upward at the swirling vultures. "I was accepting my vultures like the Indians do." Duane shook his head sideways with a grim look and returned to his shop.

The first snow of the season fell in the evening. When Ida rose in the morning, Duane was outside already with his snow blower clearing the parking lot in front of his shop. Ida came out dressed warmly to see how bad it was and out of habit she and Duane looked upward for her vultures. After a good ten minutes there were still no vultures, not one. Duane smiled, "They're gone, Ida."

"I don't see them anywhere," she said circling around the lot in the snow. She went over to her truck to see if they would come there. She couldn't find any.

"Thank God, they're gone, finally," Duane said. He screamed with joy and cheered wildly for a few minutes.

But Ida had accepted her vultures as Shanti told her and now they were gone. Maybe they were gone because she accepted them, she thought. Or would they return? And then what? Would she go through this again?

She leaned against her Chevy pickup, gazed at the bleak

gray sky and the mountains and fields around her covered in snow, and felt relieved despite her doubts. As soon as the snow was plowed, she would go to the Burger Boy and see what Shanti had to say about their leaving.

The All-Knowing Eye

Garland Duckett grabbed his navy blazer and told the secretary at McPherson's Realty he was going to lunch. He thought it best not to tell her he was heading over to Huntley Meadows to talk with God. Huntley Meadows was a nature center near his workplace in Alexandria, Virginia, so he could make it there in fifteen minutes, even if he stopped at the Krispy Kreme first to get a couple of raspberry-filled doughnuts and coffee which he planned to consume in his car. Then he would hurry out to the boardwalk built over the marsh until God made his appearance. He was convinced God resided in the body of a Great Blue Heron he saw there regularly.

Garland's first visit to Huntley Meadows was six months earlier when a client raved about its being so near the house he was trying to sell. His client bought the property and he made a nice profit. Afterwards they stopped by the park and he felt exhilarated as his client pointed out birds in the marsh pond.

When he came home with the good news about the sale, his wife, Kelly, announced she and Matt, his closest friend at McPherson's, were having an affair and were planning to move to Phoenix. His world changed in an instant and his euphoria turned to grief. He ran from the house and drove around aimlessly until he found himself at Huntley Meadows where he had felt such elation earlier. And then God in the guise of a Great Blue Heron made his first appearance.

When Garland finished his last doughnut and turned into the nearly vacant parking lot at Huntley Meadows, the sun had begun its descent. It was 3 p.m. Friday afternoon in late spring. He strode down the trail until he got to the boardwalk and continued walking to the spot where it split into two branches. Taking the less-used one, he wandered over to an expansive observation area and stopped. Resting his arms against a wooden rail, he gazed below at a large turtle in the marsh. Tall reeds surrounded the swamp which was secluded and quiet.

When he looked up, the Great Blue Heron appeared -- not six feet from him. It looked like a small, four-foot dinosaur or a prehistoric creature with large commanding golden eyes which seemed to be all-knowing the way they gazed directly at him, as though they had a deep understanding of his inner thoughts. Garland looked straight into the heron's golden eyes.

"Good, you're here again," he said to the heron whose black saber-like bill was pointed straight ahead. He sighed. "Feeling' kind of low, you know, about Kelly and Matt. I should have challenged him to a duel," he joked. Garland was an expert fencer having learned the skill when he played Hamlet in the Alexandria Little Playhouse. "I lunged at him in the office but two secretaries held me back. He sneered at me viciously."

The heron's violet-blue feathers were shimmering, accented with a light plum color around his long neck. He seemed to give Garland his full attention.

"The guy's rich but he's a thief. I told her that. Kelly said, 'You can't live in a fantasy world forever, Garland.'" He shook his head in disbelief. Garland knew he was a little strange but Kelly used to admire his uniqueness.

The heron looked at him earnestly and seemed to be sympathetic.

"Kelly changed last year. She didn't want to do the things we used to do: didn't want to fly kites in Potomac Park, didn't want to go to the theater, and didn't want to visit the cherry blossoms in the spring." Garland wiped his eyes with his sleeve. "We were married for ten years."

The heron raised his left foot as though he were about to take another step but stood there with his foot riveted in mid-air. Garland thought he should sum up.

"So here I am 35. My wife and friend gone off to Phoenix and I'm making almost daily visits to this marsh to see you. I could use some sort of sign, if you are God, to guide me." Garland was aware stranger things happen in Shakespeare's plays. He looked at the heron and pleaded, "I need your help. I'm desperate," and then stumbled back to his car.

* * *

Saturday morning Garland woke at 6 a.m., turned over and fell back to sleep dreaming about someone banging on his front door. He heard sounds from a dump truck below his window and loud male voices as he lapsed in and out of sleep. A breeze wafted into his open window bringing with it the smell of late spring gardening finally waking him at 10 a.m. The smell was pungent. Someone must be mulching in the gardens, he thought.

The breeze became stronger and the odor became more intense. When he opened his eyes he saw dirt blowing through his window. Jumping out of bed in alarm, he looked outside.

"Ah!" He put his hand near his heart. There was a pile of mulch covering the 15x15 foot plot in front of his townhouse high enough to touch with the fencing foil he kept under his bed. He reached for it, sensing trouble afoot. His view of the street was partially blocked by the mulch but he could see two kids on the sidewalk in front of his neighbor's house staring up at the enormous pile. There was a murmuring below and he suspected others were outside hidden from his view. He put the foil down and ran around the bedroom trying to find pants to throw over his shorts and a tee shirt. Cramming his feet into his Nikes and leaving the laces flapping against the floor, he took the foil with him and bounded down the stairs. As he opened the front door, a piece of paper fell at his feet. The delivery form was for the next street over, 17th Street instead of 17th Road, where he lived, and the addressee was a Chelsea Rosebery.

The mulch pile spread from the wall of his house, obliterating his garden, to the sidewalk and even as far as the tree lawn bordering the street. Astounding in scale, it completely covered the stone path to his porch, as well as the seven porch steps, preventing him from exiting his house without walking through hip-high mulch. He looked at it with wonder.

"What exactly are you planning to do with this mulch?" Marlene Higgins his next door neighbor, screamed at him over the hill of dirt, her elfin features distorted into a scowl.

"It's a mistake. I didn't order it," he gestured with his foil which he then set aside after Marlene rolled her eyes. He was reminded of Matt's sneer after he lunged at him.

"I'll say it's a mistake," she shouted. Several other townhouse residents joined her and the two kids in front of her house, mouthing words of discouragement over the mountain of mulch.

He hollered over to his neighbors thirty feet away, waving the delivery paper. "It was sent to the wrong address. It should have been delivered to a Chelsea Rosebery on 17th Street."

"How are you going to get it there?" Marlene demanded.

"I don't know," Garland stammered. "I'll call the delivery guy." He fumbled with the delivery papers and bumped his head into the storm door. "I'll call them," he promised, waving the papers at Marlene and other neighbors who had joined her to denounce the eyesore on his lawn.

"Ma'am, but I didn't order any mulch."

"Why didn't you tell the delivery man?"

"I was asleep."

"You should have been awake to receive the mulch."

"I didn't order the mulch," he said.

"Well, then what is the problem?"

"There's been a mistake. Your deliveryman dumped the mulch at the wrong address. He dumped it at 4510 17th Road and he should have dumped it at 4510 17th Street."

"Let me see, Sir. I have a copy of the shipping address here. It says 4510 17th Street. Isn't that your address?"

"No. There's a difference between Street and Road. They're different addresses."

"One minute, Sir, I have to check with my supervisor." The phone went on hold. Now there was banging on the backdoor of Garland's townhouse which continued while he grasped the phone tightly for ten minutes before he heard a click and then the recorded message, "If you would like to make a call, please hang up and dial again…"

Garland put his head in his hands. The hammering against his backdoor continued. He got up slowly to answer the door.

"What? What is it?" he said opening the backdoor. A warrior-like woman stood there, her heavyset body twice as large as Garland's who was a trim six feet.

"Garland Duckett?"

"Yes."

"I'm Pearl Burgher, Chair of the Condo Covenants Committee for the Fox Ridge townhouses."

He heard of her and knew she wasn't someone to cross.

"You are in extreme violation of Section 34 of the Condo covenants document for the Fox Ridge townhouses," she continued.

"But I was sleeping. How could I commit a violation when I was sleeping?" He felt overwhelmed and wished Kelly was

21

around to deal with this absurd situation. He had enough trouble coping with the ordinary.

"What a monstrosity. It's an eyesore and a health hazard. You have 24 hours to get rid of that obscene pile of mulch on your front lawn."

"How am I going to get someone here on the weekend?"

"Something you should have considered when you took delivery."

"I was asleep when it was delivered."

"What kind of person can sleep through a ton of manure being dumped on him?"

Garland thought about that while Pearl searched through her tote bag vigorously. The image of Kelly and Matt on a golf course in Arizona passed through his mind.

"Get rid of the mulch or you'll be charged $50 each day it stays there," Pearl said and slapped him with a Condo Covenants Committee summons. Garland closed the door, his pulse racing. Sitting down in his kitchen for a few minutes, he did deep breathing exercises from the Yoga classes Kelly insisted he take early in their marriage. He could not bear to call the shipping company again but was in a quandary about what he should do.

Chelsea Rosebery. She was the answer; she ordered the mulch. He looked through his blinds and could not see anyone else waiting to accost him so he grabbed his nylon windbreaker and went to find her house.

He rang the bell on the front portico of 4510 17th Street. What a mansion, he thought. He remembered when it was for sale eight years ago with seven bedrooms, four baths, a swimming pool, Jacuzzi, finished basement, finished attic. The door opened slowly and a tall, willowy woman was visible behind the screen door.

"Chelsea Rosebery?"

"Yes?"

"Hello, I'm Garland Duckett," he said.

"What a lovely name -- Garland," she said in a hushed tone.

"I have your mulch," he said.

"Oh, drive around the back and pile it next to the greenhouse." She opened the door and came outside.

"No. I mean. Your mulch is on my front lawn. I live on 17th Road and the deliveryman made a mistake and dumped the mulch on my front lawn." Garland emboldened his tenor voice.

"Oh, dear." She paused putting her long thin fingers on her cheek. Garland noticed how clear and flawless her skin was and how symmetrical her features appeared. She would be a good Rosalind in *As You Like It*. "What should we do?"

"I think we have quite a dilemma here. It's a lot of mulch."

"Oh, but I need that much. I'm making a wildlife nature preserve in my backyard. Would you like to see it?"

Chelsea's voice mesmerized Garland. It was soft and light and faded in and out like a whisper. He thought of Kelly's assertive voice and then answered, "Yes. Yes, I would." Chelsea led him around back. She was as tall as he was and moved gracefully as she walked around in a gossamer full-length lavender gown imprinted with small gold butterflies.

"What beautiful landscaping," he said to her as they walked into her backyard.

"Yes, but I want it to be natural. I want to create a marsh to attract birds and wildlife," she said in a breathless hush. "There are five acres here."

"It sounds very nice. I frequently visit the marshlands at Huntley Meadows to see the birds there," he said.

"I love Huntley Meadows," she answered. She could have been a sorceress the way her hazel eyes with their golden specs and her faint smile held his gaze. Kelly had agitating eyes which darted around her surroundings like gnats.

"I'm building a backyard habitat. I have the perfect land for it," Chelsea said looking across the forested land and meadows behind her house. "Soon the wildflowers will be in bloom." Twenty-five bird feeders and birdhouses were spread throughout her property. "I simply have to do add a marshy area and I'm sure I can then attract some rare creatures right here."

"You can make your own little Huntley Meadows in your backyard," he encouraged her.

"Yes, that's what I was envisioning. And let me show you my sunroom." She led him up the steps onto an expansive deck.

Garland was enthralled when he saw the marbleized deep-green Jacuzzi hot tub in the corner of the deck. He went over to it and ran his fingers over the smooth ceramic interior.

"It helps my aching body in the morning," Chelsea said. He smiled and couldn't help picturing her naked for a brief moment. She was quite a lovely, ephemeral woman. She led him through French doors to a sunroom like none he had ever seen as a realtor. It was as large as his whole downstairs with arched, designer windows everywhere, and several birding scopes set up around the room directed toward the backyard.

"This is amazing. Truly amazing," he said.

"But we're forgetting about the mulch problem," Chelsea reminded him.

"Problems are made to be solved," he said with a cavalier wave of his hand. "It's just mulch. We'll get it over here some way."

"Would you like some wine and cheese?" she said, "It's getting close to lunchtime."

"Sounds wonderful," he answered. "I think I deserve a little relief after the traumas of the morning."

"I'm so sorry this happened to you," she said.

Garland joked, "The Condo Covenants Committee at Fox

Ridge is on my case for this. You'd think it was World War III."

"But I don't want to cause you any trouble."

"No," he said accepting his wine in a beautifully etched crystal goblet. "If we can find someone with a dump truck we can solve the problem."

"My landscaper has a dump truck."

"Excellent. That would help a lot."

"I'll call my landscaper to pick it up and bring it over here."

"That would be the fastest solution," Garland said, pleased Chelsea had provided the means to resolve the issue so effortlessly. He began to relax lounging in her sunroom while enjoying the wine and cheese. Over the next half-hour they talked about the marshlands and consumed the entire bottle of wine. Chelsea opened another bottle of White Zinfandel with its rose blush and poured it in his glass.

"Delightful," he said feeling quite drunk.

"I plan to build a wetland stretching from the river birch to the sycamore," she continued, "I hope to attract birds, turtles, foxes, beavers…"

Yes, and maybe rats, mice and other vermin, Garland, the realtor, thought. But he said, "How fascinating, a wildlife habitat right here." If his Fox Ridge neighbors realized what Chelsea was planning in their backyard, the mulch pile in front of his house would not be their biggest concern.

"And do you live here alone?" he asked.

"Yes, except when my daughter visits. She goes to Berkeley, my alma mater. My ex-husband is long gone. But he left me with a nice settlement." She waved her arm around the place. "He wasn't about to spend his life with an aging poet."

"Oh, you're a poet. Remember what Antony said about Cleopatra, 'Age cannot wither her, nor custom stale her infinite variety,'" Garland said.

"You are so generous with your Shakespearean perceptions,"

Chelsea said smiling, her eyebrows raised in surprise at his dramatic prowess.

Women were so concerned about their age, Garland thought. She looked fine to him, maybe five years older than he was. He was now deeply drunk and Kelly and Matt receded far into the background of his mind. Chelsea moved elegantly around the room in her lavender gown. How fitting she's a poet, he thought.

"Your dress is the same color as the white zinfandel," he said.

"What a wonderful metaphor," she said glancing at her dress and then the wine.

She sat next to him, glass in hand and began reciting one of her poems. He heard words like "tangerine," "dancing," "blossom," "wreath," "mingling," "lyre," "altar" but he had lost the ability to tie them together in any meaningful way.

"Beautiful, beautiful," he said.

"It's so rare to find a man who can listen so intently to poetry," she said moving close to him to whisper the last line. "Because the chalice is full and Athena beckons."

He felt his pulse beating now as he realized she had nothing on under her multilayer diaphanous dress. Leaning toward him, her breasts were visible. He had a strong impulse to throw his head into her cleavage and was trying hard to think about the mulch, the heron, his ex-wife, and his former friend. But he was overcome by the curves of her breasts, her waist and abdomen as she continued to recite an avalanche of verses which made no sense to him except for occasional images the words evoked, "liquid gold," pomegranate," "pale blue sky". He was trying hard to recover himself when she said. "Not so bad for a fiftyish poet, is it?"

My God, she is nearly twenty years older than me, he thought. He envisioned Matt and Kelly laughing at him. Here he was nearly swirling into her breasts. Think about the mulch.

Visualize. Visualize a pile of mulch in front of your house. But he was in a state of intoxication and dreaminess which was entrenched and promised to get worse as Chelsea reached over to fill his wine glass. Abruptly, he put the glass down.

"I must go," he said, "the mulch."

"Oh, yes, the mulch," she said.

"The mulch," they both said in unison.

Garland got up, staggering, bumping into scopes and floor cushions. He groped his way to the deck, gazing back at the poet following like Athena behind him, her lavender gown blowing in the breeze. The fresh air helped to revive him slightly but he stumbled across Chelsea's lawn waving at her, occasionally murmuring "Mulch" and she in return called after him, "The mulch, yes."

Garland arose at 5 a.m. Sunday to the smell of the mulch now permeating his townhouse. He decided to go into work instead of facing the scrutiny of Pearl Burgher who started her incessant walks with her dog at 6 a.m. Before he went, he shoveled some of the mulch into a trash bag and put it into the trunk of his car.

After spending an hour on a few pending contracts at McPherson's Realty, Garland left the office and drove over to Huntley Meadows. The parking lot at the marshland was full as the sun ascended. He walked briskly on the trail leading to the boardwalk and then stopped at the spot where the sacred heron usually appeared. After twenty minutes of waiting, Garland saw the heron wading through the marsh toward him. He stopped several feet from the boardwalk and stood silently staring at Garland in the morning sunlight looking so beautiful with the lavender hue around his neck.

"I had quite an adventure yesterday," he said to the heron, "But I managed to get through it, managed to deal with a lot of unsavory characters. And then I got out of a pretty sticky situation with an attractive older woman. I've been in enough Shakespearean comedies to recognize a comic situation when I see it."

"Oh, look, Mommy," a little girl said coming over to the heron. Garland wasn't prepared for this infringement on his personal space with God. He looked at the child and then decided to ignore these people who, he reasoned, he would never see again, and continued talking to the heron.

"The mulch was a perfect sign. I felt a lot better yesterday visiting with Chelsea. I brought some mulch as an offering," he said to the heron, "It's organic."

The little girl's mother had now joined her and glared at Garland as he conversed with the heron. Garland opened the bag of mulch with the heron still staring at him, his foot lifted transfixed in space. He spilled the mulch into the marsh in front of the heron and the bird immediately spread out his wings and flew away, grazing Garland's head.

"Ah!" the little girl screamed.

"What's wrong with you?" her mother yelled at Garland.

Garland stood riveted to the spot for the moment. He walked away slowly wondering why God left so abruptly. He consoled himself by thinking maybe God planned to appear at another spot to lead him on the right path.

* * *

The next morning Chelsea's landscape company came early and began shoveling the mulch into a dump truck with a back hoe. After he saw from his window they were making good progress, he went out to observe with the rest of the neighborhood. When they got the mulch loaded and had hosed down his yard and sidewalks, there was no sign the mulch was ever there. He considered walking to Chelsea's to thank her for getting the job done so efficiently but the image of her bare breasts floated into his head and he decided it was better to forget the whole episode, lest he lose his self-control. He could imagine Kelly and Matt's sarcasm if they ever knew he was with a woman old enough to be his mother.

Garland went to Huntley Meadows several times the next week but the sacred heron was not there. He clung to the hope God would appear somewhere else to lead him down the right path. By Friday, he decided not to return to Huntley Meadows; it seemed pointless to visit without God there.

Two weeks later he was drinking white zinfandel on his deck to lift his spirits. The heron had not appeared to him and he was depressed. The wine made him feel drowsy and relaxed. Chelsea's favorite wine, he thought, taking another sip. Half-asleep he moved in and out of his dreams, aware he was on the deck, but seeing images of Kelly with Matt, kites blowing in the air, the Great Blue heron, he and Matt bicycling over a rugged trail, Chelsea gliding across her deck in her lavender gown, the plum-colored feathers on the heron's neck and Chelsea again.

He woke suddenly, the latter images still with him. He felt an intense desire to hear Chelsea recite her poetry. He poured the wine and thought "Her voice was ever soft, gentle and low, an excellent thing in women." Chelsea was so whimsical and Kelly and Matt were "manured with industry." Lines from the plays he had memorized were rising to the top of his consciousness. Chelsea was a "very" Chelsea and he was a "very" Garland like Antony and Cleopatra. Sipping his wine, he felt proud of his own ability to pull words and thoughts at will from Shakespearean plays. Images of Chelsea's graceful hands, sensuous lips, flowing robes, rounded breasts floated in and out. Why should he care about her age? She was a rare woman, the kind one usually encounters on stage in a play.

He needed to take action or else he would become like Hamlet. Rising from his lounge chair a little tipsy, he sleepwalked over to 17th Street carrying with him a full bottle of white zinfandel. It was three weeks since the mulch delivery and he should inquire about the backyard habitat.

Chelsea opened the door and greeted him on the portico dressed alluringly in a long white silk gown.

"You look like the Empress Josephine," he said. She smiled and seemed pleased to see him.

"It's my tribute to Christina Rossetti," she said. "Did you notice the garlands in my hair?"

He blushed at the play on his name as she turned her head to reveal fresh violets woven through her elegantly-styled hair.

"Very nice," he said circling behind her to examine her intricate hair arrangement, his heart pounding against his chest.

"You move so gracefully, like a dancer," she said.

"I'm a fencer," Garland said assuming the "on guard" position with the wine bottle acting as the sword.

"Fencing, how gallant. It suits you," she said half-whispering. Garland glowed at the praise.

"I've come over to see the wildlife habitat," Garland said.

"It's wonderful," she said clasping her hands together over her bosom.

Garland entered the house through the front door. The living room had carved molding on the ceilings, Grecian vases, colorful silk pillows, large medieval tapestries, the fragrance of fresh fruit in golden bowls, and the sound of haunting flute music in the background. Garland turned slowly in a circle to take everything in. Matt or Kelly would never appreciate the sensuousness of this room, he thought.

Chelsea led him into the sunroom with its powerful scopes now looking out to the new marsh completely transforming the backyard.

"Reminds me of Huntley Meadows," he said with pleasure.

"Come out," she said. He put the bottle on the coffee table

and went with Chelsea out to the deck and then into the back-yard. They walked over the freshly cut grass toward the meadow which was blooming with spring wild flowers. Chelsea picked some and twirled toward Garland. He smiled at her, beginning to feel the hypnotic sense he did the last time he was with her. He went over to the new marsh which had a small boardwalk built over it. Chelsea walked toward it like a Greek goddess.

"Fantastic," he said shaking his head in astonishment.

"And you should see the wildlife it attracts," she said, "This morning I saw two solitary sandpipers on this very spot." She looked at him with a subtle smile which he shyly returned.

"I would love to hear your poems," he implored.

Chelsea began reciting one of her poems, her soft voice so soothing, so comforting to Garland. He looked into her eyes and a vivid image of the heron drifted into his thoughts. When she finished, he said, "I have seen a Great Blue Heron at Huntley Meadows who has these all-knowing eyes."

"All-knowing eyes, how wonderful!" she whispered so near his ear he could feel her breath.

Chasing the Loon

Mrs. Henny was preparing to go to bed early because she had a busy schedule planned for Mother's Day. First she would walk to the Baptist church a block from her son Kevin's house in Arlington and introduce herself to the congregation at the morning service. Then her son had agreed, although reluctantly, to take her to visit her sister, Grace, in the Spring Garden Assisted Living Center in Maryland across the Potomac.

"Mother's Day falls right during peak bird migration in Washington," Kevin had pleaded. "This is the high point of the year for birders." Mrs. Henny was unmoved by his assertion and insisted he take her to visit Grace. She wanted to be with her sister now. Grace would know what she was going through—being uprooted, homeless. Grace didn't speak much after her last stroke, but Mrs. Henny needed the comfort of being near her. She shuddered to think she might find herself in one of those homes someday. She was 76 and wasn't getting any younger, although she kept current with the latest medical advice at Dr. Murphy's where she had worked as a receptionist. Yes, she was a little overweight but that was because she was five feet tall and you could hardly eat a decent meal without gaining weight at her age.

She had felt a bit dizzy since she moved in with Kevin a week ago. His house seemed so unfamiliar. She looked around at her bedroom as she knelt down to say her evening prayers.

On the bedside table there was a ceramic bowl of stones with a jet of water circulating over them continually. On the wall next to the bureau was a painting of strange Japanese symbols—calligraphy, Kevin called it. Another picture of row after row of different types of butterflies hung over the cedar chest directly across from the foot of the bed. When she woke in the morning, she thought a swarm of butterflies was heading straight toward her. She felt like she was in an Asian rain forest or something.

Kevin worked for the National Park Service and had decorated the whole house with animals and nature objects. When she raised her head toward heaven to pray, gazing back at her was a picture of a loon swimming in a misty lake which hung above her bed. The loon had a dark green head and red eyes. Lord, she thought, that red eye staring out at me is making me nervous. With its neck slightly raised, its bill looked like a dagger. Examining its black-checkered back, white breast, and white collar with vertical stripes she became slightly dizzy again.

She gave up praying and climbed into bed. Then her body jerked as she heard a sound coming from Kevin's bedroom. He was in there with his girlfriend, Denise, imitating the loon and doing who knows what. She grimaced as she turned over to try to sleep while hearing what sounded like a crazy lady laughing like a lunatic. Lord, if this doesn't push me over the edge, what will, she thought.

* * *

Mrs. Henny waited at the kitchen table for Kevin to finish his morning Tai Chi exercises in his Meditation garden. She was still dressed in her church clothes, a three-piece orange and black print suit with bolero. "My, you look like a monarch butterfly this morning," one of the women at the Baptist church said to her after the service—which Mrs. Henny thought was just plain rude confirming her impression that there were a lot of snooty people in Arlington.

Hurry it up with that nonsense, she thought, as she waited for Kevin. She opened a compact to refresh her makeup. She had a habit of expressing her emotions with a variety of facial grimaces and the lines in her face were more visible by her use of heavy face powder to hide her accumulating old age blemishes.

Mrs. Henny needed Kevin to drive her to the assisted living center because she had lost her Virginia Driver's license a month earlier after she was charged in a four-car collision when exiting a shopping center on Route 1 in Alexandria. The accident snarled traffic for hours. She could still feel the jolt that caused everyone involved to claim whiplash. It was her fault. She wasn't concentrating on her driving, as she should have. Earlier in the day Dr. Murphy had informed her he was transferring his practice to an HMO and would have to abolish her job.

"It's time for you to think about retirement anyway," he said. She loved being a medical receptionist and had mastered the art of small talk on illness and disease with Dr. Murphy's patients who she knew by their first names. She didn't want to retire and her Social Security would not cover the rent in her Alexandria apartment and all of her other living expenses. After their seventh phone conversation on her finances, she heard Kevin give a long, drawn-out sigh and then say, "You had better move in with me."

"Hello, Mrs. Henny. How are you on this beautiful Sunday morning?" Denise said coming into the kitchen.

"I've been better," Mrs. Henny responded.

Denise visited Kevin almost daily and was so nice it made Mrs. Henny suspicious. Denise was almost as tall as Kevin and looked very healthy from living out in the woods so much with the Park Service. She got granola, yogurt and strawberries from the refrigerator. This seemed to be the only choice for breakfast. Mrs. Henny had already eaten, making do with a single piece of toast and a cup of instant coffee.

Now she heard another strange sound, this time from the garden.

"What is going on out there?" she asked Denise.

"He's chanting," she laughed. "He chants his Buddhist prayers on Sunday morning.

"Kevin is a Buddhist?" Mrs. Henny asked.

"Kevin is an ascetic monk." Denise laughed. "He's quite spiritual."

"Kevin stopped going to church in high school," Mrs. Henny corrected her. Kevin was raised to be a good Southern Baptist but he quit when he was in high school just to spite her and make her worry about whether he was going to end in hell. He didn't believe anything she believed after he started high school and laughed at all of her favorite sayings as though they were supposed to be funny. But she couldn't complain about Kevin. He had taken her in.

"Oh, he doesn't believe in formal religion. He has his own rituals," Denise rambled on while preparing her breakfast.

Kevin came in from the garden dressed in Karate attire and sprang into a threatening stance with one leg bent forward and the other stretched behind. His right hand was raised above his head and the other was bent at his waist holding an Asian sword. Mrs. Henny put her hand on her heart and jumped a little in her chair. He smiled, bowed to her and then came over and kissed her on the cheek.

"Happy Mother's Day, Mother," he said. He was a tall, slender, graceful man.

"Thank you, Kevin," she said, "Don't forget you promised to take me to see your Aunt Grace today."

"How could I forget?" he said sitting next to her smiling broadly.

"Oh, lord, Kevin." Mrs. Henny said, "You would be better off going to church on Sunday morning instead of jumping around in the garden."

"I have my church right here," Kevin made a sweeping gesture all around him.

"Not one picture of Jesus in this house," Mrs. Henny said.

"But I have a bronze Buddha in the hall," Kevin laughed.

"Well, I'm taking down the loon from over my bed and replacing it with Jesus," Mrs. Henny said, "I'm not about to pray to a duck every night."

"Alright, but I think you're making a big mistake. The loon is the oldest bird in the world and knows all the secrets of the universe."

"You shouldn't joke about religion, Kevin," Mrs. Henny said.

"I'm serious. The loon is a much more spiritual sight than any minister I've ever seen," Kevin said.

"There I have to agree with you." Denise patted his hand.

"Kevin, don't be sinful. You're talking about a bird and I'm talking about our Lord and Savior, Jesus Christ. I'm taking down the loon picture this evening and putting up Jesus."

"Suit yourself, Mother," Kevin said, scanning the Sunday paper.

An hour later Mrs. Henny hoisted her short, rotund body into the passenger seat of Kevin's Jeep Cherokee SUV and prepared to visit her sister at the home.

"You know Mother's Day falls right during peak migration in Washington," Kevin said, his khaki clothes resembling a Safari outfit.

"You've said that a hundred times this week, Kevin. You've seen all the birds in Virginia over and over again," she said, "It won't hurt you to visit your Aunt Grace once in a while."

"But there's a Pacific Loon off-territory in the Potomac," Kevin said, "I've never seen a Pacific Loon."

"How do you know there's a Pacific Loon here, if you haven't seen it?" Mrs. Henny asked.

"It's on the Web. When one birder sees something unusual, they post it on the Web," Kevin said.

"Well, I'm sorry Kevin. Grace is expecting me. And I need to be with my sister today. I've had a difficult month, Lord knows."

"I'm taking you," Kevin said starting the car, "but I want to stop at the overlook on the George Washington Parkway to see if I can spot the Pacific Loon in the Potomac. He's supposed to be there. It'll only take five minutes."

"Well, O.K., if it's only five minutes. I guess Grace can wait another five minutes. The poor thing spends most of her life waiting in that home."

"I may have to chase him up the Potomac and stop at several overlooks. So five minutes at each overlook," Kevin said.

"Oh, now it's ten or fifteen minutes late," she grumbled. But she was willing to wait for him while he checked for the peculiar bird.

Kevin drove through Arlington and got on the parkway. Strange chanting music was on the car tape deck. Mrs. Henny's eyes were stretched wide open. The Eastern chants were unsettling to her Baptist ears. "Amazing Grace" would be so much more comforting, she thought. When they got to the overlook, Kevin pulled in and stopped the car.

"Stay here, I'll just be a few minutes," he said. He got out of the car with his binoculars. She checked her watch. Kevin appeared to know some of the other birders who were already there and began talking to them while everyone looked down into the Potomac.

Fifteen minutes later, Mrs. Henny looked at her watch and shook her head. The birders, including her son, were still searching the Potomac with their binoculars. She was getting restless. The chanting was still on the tape deck. From time to time a gong would go off giving her a start. She looked around the parking area and saw wild blue-violet chicory off to the side. Wouldn't Grace love to see wildflowers? Cooped up in the assisted living home, I bet she probably hadn't seen chicory since she got there, she thought.

She opened the door and stumbled out of the SUV with her black leather purse and pumps, giving the door a good slam. Heading over to the chicory, she glanced at her son at the other end of the overlook, still engaged with his friends in seeking out the Pacific Loon. She began picking chicory and collected quite a mound of it before she turned around toward the car. Her mouth dropped open as she saw the rear end of the SUV tearing out of the lot onto the parkway. Her son had left her there on the overlook. He had run off with his friends and no one but her and two men in black leather on motorcycles remained. She dropped the chicory over the parking lot and stood there unable to move. Her son abandoned her on the George Washington Parkway on Mother's Day. You couldn't get a bus or cab from here or even walk down the parkway without risking your life. And she knew there was no good way for him to turn around on the parkway either. She was speechless, shaking.

A car entered the overlook parking lot and blew its horn at her to move. She stepped back and the car ran over the chicory that was lying on the ground. A young couple got out of the car and went to look at the Potomac River below. They soon lost interest in the scene and began groping each other.

"Oh, Lord," Mrs. Henny said.

"What did you say?" the young woman said turning around and approaching Mrs. Henny.

"Nothing," she said. In the meantime the two motorcyclists left the overlook and headed for the parkway.

The young woman, who was what Mrs. Henny would call trailer-park trashy, was wearing jeans cut so low her whole belly was showing. She came over to Mrs. Henny and asked, "Can I borrow a twenty from you?"

"I don't have that much," Mrs. Henny said wishing her purse would disappear.

The young girl looked around, "Where's your car? What are you doing here?" she asked.

Mrs. Henny replied, "I'm looking for the Pacific Loon down there in the Potomac. It's a rare bird."

The girl looked over at her boyfriend and motioned with her head. He nodded at her with a menacing smirk.

A Ford Explorer drove into the parking lot and pulled into a space near Mrs. Henny. A group of five birders dressed mainly in shades of beige bolted out of the SUV; four of them headed toward the overlook rim. One middle-aged woman with a baseball cap from Costa Rica got a scope and tripod and crossed in front of Mrs. Henny.

"We're chasing the loon," she said to Mrs. Henny.

"So am I," Mrs. Henny said impulsively and began taking short, brisk steps to stay with the group as they rushed to the overlook rim. Out of the corner of her eye she could see the young couple staring at her.

"Did you see it?" the woman with the scope said.

"No, not yet," Mrs. Henny replied.

"Well, let me reposition the scope and see," she said, smiling at Mrs. Henny.

Mrs. Henny stood close to her and tried to merge in with the bird group, despite the contrast between her Mother's Day dress and their absurd clothing and gear. The birders had their white socks rolled over their beige pants legs. One woman who looked to be 80 was wearing two hats, a larger rigid-brimmed hat super-imposed on a smaller floppy-brimmed hat. She was as thin as one of Dr. Murphy's patients on life support and looked as though the next wind would blow her away. But she lifted her binoculars and scoured the Potomac with the rest of them. A tall lanky man had on a sweatshirt with a colorful picture of Woody Woodpecker. Mrs. Henny had never seen such a bizarre collection of people in one place. You would think they just arrived from fly fishing in Minnesota what with those pockets slapped all over their shirts, pants and vests. But she felt she was safer with this group than with the others on the overlook. And the group was concentrating on searching the Potomac for the loon so diligently they never seemed to notice she was dressed in her Sunday clothes.

"Charlotte, did you get the scope focused on the loons down there?" the Woody Woodpecker man yelled.

"Yes, I see them," the middle-aged woman with the scope responded, "but I don't see the Pacific Loon yet."

Mrs. Henny noticed the young couple creeping over her way again.

"Do you want to take a look?" Charlotte said to Mrs. Henny, offering her a look through the scope setup on a tripod.

"O.K. Thank you," Mrs. Henny said. She couldn't see much except a lot of fuzzy ducks. Lord, she thought. How did she get in this position?

"Do you see the loons?" Charlotte asked, "You can focus it better for yourself by turning this dial."

Mrs. Henny moved the focus a bit and said, "Yes. Yes. There they are—the loons. They look like the picture I have in my bedroom."

"They are late flying north this year," Charlotte said. "Give us your best loon call, Bob," she yelled to the tall lanky man.

Bob raised his pitch and sang, "Ha-oo-oo. Ha-oo-oo. Ha-oo-oo."

"Lord, it sounds like a crazy old lady. I should be able to do that," Mrs. Henny said and the birding group laughed at her remark.

"Go ahead," Charlotte said, "You try."

Mrs. Henny, who sang in the choir of her Baptist church in Alexandria for years, took a deep breath and belted out, "Uh-Uh-Uh-Uh-Uh. Uh-Uh-Uh-Uh-Uh," at a very high frequency, imitating the sounds coming out of Kevin's bedroom last night.

The birders applauded.

"Wow! Some impression," Bob said.

Charlotte was hunched over her scope and said, "Look, I think I see the Pacific Loon down there. I think your call brought in the Pacific Loon," she chuckled.

Everyone focused their scopes and binoculars down on the Potomac.

"Which one is it?" Mrs. Henny asked, looking into Charlotte's scope. Charlotte described the field marks for the Pacific Loon and showed Mrs. Henny the pictures in her National Geographic field guide.

"I think I see it," Mrs. Henny said. She then felt a tap on her shoulder. Mrs. Henny was startled thinking it was the threatening couple but it was her son, Kevin. In the background, she saw the young couple leaving the overlook in their car.

"Mother, I'm so sorry. I didn't know you got out of the car. I thought I saw the loon fly towards the next overlook and I wanted to get there quickly before it flew off again. I was so focused on the loon I guess I forgot about you."

"Hi Kevin," Bob yelled over. Kevin waved.

"Oh, are you Kevin's mother?" Charlotte asked Mrs. Henny.

"Yes, he's my son, Kevin. He always did like birds and frogs and bugs and crawling creatures," Mrs. Henny said.

"That sounds like Kevin," Charlotte said.

The other birders laughed. However Kevin looked

disheartened. Mrs. Henny thought he might start explaining how he abandoned his mother on the overlook, so she said, "Did you see the Pacific Loon, Kevin?"

"No. I never did," he said.

"It's down there now. Go ahead. Go ahead. Look through Charlotte's scope," Mrs. Henny said. Charlotte smiled and offered her scope to Kevin who peered into it.

"Yes! Yes! I see it down there!"

He stayed with his birding friends for a few minutes while Mrs. Henny chatted with Charlotte. Then he put his arm around his mother and said, "Come on, Mother. Let's go visit Aunt Grace."

"Kevin's taking me to see my sister—his Aunt Grace," Mrs. Henny said to Charlotte. "He's such a good son."

Mrs. Henny said her goodbyes to the birders, who teased her about her piercing loon call and encouraged her to go birding again. Charlotte said learning birdsongs was very difficult and was something the group needed. Mrs. Henny had a good memory for song and was thinking she might like to help out the group.

Kevin took her hand and walked her to the car. For the first time since her retirement she felt a sense of relief, a lightness floating over her.

Searching for Life on Mars

Nelson Mayfield was extremely fatigued. Last week he turned thirty which meant he had already lived the average life span for a person with his lung condition. He searched for his next breath.

Lying in his recliner, he observed a squirrel outside his bedroom window sprinting up the trunk of a large oak tree. Its nimble body turned first one way, then pirouetted and fearlessly scampered upward to the topmost branches. Perhaps, my soul will pass on to a squirrel, Nelson mused. How carefree to be a squirrel. They were so fleet of foot with so much energy, so agile and so bold.

"Nelson, sweetheart, how're you feeling this morning, dear?" His mother burst into his room with her usual cheer. He was disheartened when he saw she was wearing her large-brimmed red hat. It reminded him she was traveling today. Her company in the Tech Corridor of Northern Virginia frequently had off-site weekend strategy sessions.

"I'm O.K. A little tired," he said. His once handsome face had thinned into shadowy hollows and his blond hair was trimmed in a buzz cut for easier maintenance.

"I've asked Serena and her mother to stay over the weekend so at least one of them is in the house at all times while I'm away.

"O.K., Mother. Don't worry about me."

"Are you sure you're alright?" his mother came over to the recliner and put her arms around him. She was a corporate executive working long hours which frequently left Nelson in the inept hands of Serena, who spent most of her time in her basement live-in quarters visiting with her extended family—cousins, uncles, aunts. He had met more members of her family than his own. Nelson never mentioned this to his mother who had struggled with caring for him and going to work for all these years. His parents divorced when he was in high school—probably because of him, he suspected.

"Go. Go," he said kissing her. She gave him a long hug. He felt terrible this morning but didn't want to complicate her life any more than he had already.

When she left, he dragged himself out of the recliner and into his power-driven wheelchair. He motored over to his computer to get absorbed in something scientific, something emotionless. First, he opened his CD player and put in five CDs of Gregorian and medieval chants, which he found soothing as background music.

Nelson was an ace at computers and had achieved high honors in mathematics at Johns Hopkins when he was in better health, nearly completing his Ph.D. until his disease worsened and prevented his continuing at the university. If he were not chronically sick, he would have made a nice career in mathematics, but instead he used his skills to amuse himself with his computer.

He planned to use his own programmed software called "Zoom" to enlarge the live photos from Mars. Not only did his program enlarge sections of the surface of Mars, but it used advanced mathematical formulae to refine the enlarged pictures to eliminate graininess. He suspected he had built a better model than NASA to peruse the Martian photos.

He logged into his favorite scientific chat room on the Internet with his ID, "Airsupply". "Hi. I just logged on," he typed to his scientific Internet cronies. He coughed up phlegm and threw the tissue in the large wastebasket next to his desk.

There were several people conversing about the Mars photos; nothing too interesting. He opened another computer window to start examining the photos. Using "Zoom" he zeroed in on a picture and entertained himself for about twenty minutes looking around the surface of Mars. Out of the corner of his eye, he saw the chat room had become very active so he scrolled through to see what was so important.

He read, "Get out of the chat room, Whizkid," "What a lot of bunk," and "This is for serious scientists." He scrolled back to see what Whizkid had said and found a line, "There's some kind of animal on Mars. What is it?" Then a response, "You must be drinking, Whizkid." A response from Whizkid read "I know what I see."

Nelson laughed at the scientists' furor over nothing. "What is the URL address, Whizkid?" he typed, while he tried to control a coughing spell. He was called Whizkid, too, when he was a young, budding scientist and he never appreciated being dismissed by condescending adults.

"What?" Whizkid responded.

"The address at the top of the window," he typed.

Eventually, an elaborate address appeared on his screen and Nelson quickly entered it displaying a section of the Mars surface with a large crater surrounded by numerous rocks and crevices. NASA had installed a live camera on this section of Mars. He surveyed the entire area and didn't see anything amiss. He returned to the chat room and typed in "Whizkid, what does it look like to you?" In a few minutes he got a response, "Like a squirrel or a prairie dog darting around."

A squirrel? Preposterous but he chuckled as he thought about the playful squirrel that morning. He wheezed trying to catch his breath.

A squirrel on Mars was of course ludicrous. Still he had nothing better to do, so he decided to pursue modifications in his "Zoom" software he was contemplating for a while to check out what the Whizkid observed.

He heard a knock on his door. "Mr. Mayfield, I brought you your lunch," Serena said.

"Come in."

Serena entered the room avoiding eye contact with Nelson.

"Don't worry, Serena. I promise I won't die on your watch," Nelson joked.

"Oh, you are too young," she answered with feigned assurance.

Nelson suspected this was why Serena had a number of her relatives over while his mother traveled and he didn't blame her.

"Put it there," he said, "I'll eat it later." Serena paused as though she thought she should provide greater service. She had very prominent cheek bones, large eyes and enormous lips, evoking the look of an ancient Incan, although she was twenty eight. After she turned twenty five, her mother had stopped trying to find her a husband, thinking she was probably too exotic in appearance to attract a man in this country.

"Is it church music?" she smiled as she removed the garbage bag in the wastebasket and put in another.

"Yes, I've become very religious, Serena." He looked over at his statue of Buddha in the corner. Serena followed his eyes and looked perplexed.

"I'm hedging my bets," he said, "I've decided to believe in all religions in case one of them is right."

"Oh," she laughed and waved her hand at him as she hurried from the room.

He decided to have a little soup now that she had interrupted his programming, but he had difficulty swallowing it and returned to his computer. He continued working for another hour, coughing every few minutes and refilling the wastebasket with phlegm and blood-laced tissues.

After pausing a few minutes from his fatigue, he shook off his weariness and refocused on developing his code adding several new formulae that would further refine his "Zoom" program. When he became consumed by the computer logic, he lost all sense of time and bodily comforts. His breathing was becoming strained as he neglected his medicine and lunch but his mind was operating at an optimal level.

Finally he was ready to try the new program on the Mars photos "zooming in" on every inch of the frame. His eyes were fixed to his screen to see if there was anything unusual in the live photo. For an hour he stared at the screen as his program surveyed the surface of Mars.

When the program completed, he produced nothing, nothing. He knew this was a foolish pursuit but was still disheartened and wrote a message in the Chat Room to Whizkid. "No squirrels, Whizkid."

A message was typed by Whizkid saying, "He's still there to the left of the big round crater."

Other messages crept in. "What's wrong with you, Airsupply?" "Why are you even looking?" "You're encouraging him, Airsupply."

Nelson sighed. He was running out of options. He looked out the window and saw a squirrel jumping from branch to branch as though he were showing off for his audience. Who knows, he thought. Perhaps if he used differential geometry, the results might be different. He began feverishly working on this new idea, but after an hour he was interrupted by a knock on the door.

"Yes?" he said.

"It's Serena's Uncle Ernesto," a crusty voice answered. The

door opened slightly and a short, muscular man with a handlebar moustache poked his head in. "I come for the tray."

"O.K. Come in," Nelson said. He remembered that Uncle Ernesto had plastered the ceiling in the bathroom for his mother.

"Could I get something for you?" Uncle Ernesto said lingering.

"How about a new lung?" Nelson said with a smirk.

"Well, I know a man in Mexico who might be able to help you?" Uncle Ernesto arched his bushy eyebrows.

Nelson laughed, "Good one."

"This is cathedral music," Uncle Ernesto gestured toward the CD player.

"I've become a monk," Nelson said.

Uncle Ernesto came over to him with the tray in one arm and placed his other large beefy hand on Nelson's shoulder bending down toward his wheelchair. "Play mariachi music, man. This music is for Sunday morning."

"Well, I'm celebrating Sunday early," he said folding his two hands in prayer and bowing his head. Uncle Ernesto laughed and left with the tray.

Nelson continued with programming his new algorithm and in another hour tried it out on the surface of Mars.

Nothing.

He pounded his programming manual against his desk.

"S--t!" he said, nothing, not even an unusual rock or something. His mathematical nature drove him to find answers but he thought it was time to quit. He was tiring himself out.

He responded to the Whizkid "There's nothing there, Whizkid. No squirrel."

"You mention a squirrel again, Airsupply, and you're officially banned from this Chat Room." "Don't be monopolizing our time with this nonsense." "Get a life."

He laughed, wishing he could get a life. A few tears rolled

down his cheek and fell onto his keyboard. He heard a tapping on the door and quickly dried his eyes. "Come in." It was Serena with her mother, Mama Rosario, bringing in his dinner. He had met Mama Rosario before. She reminded him of a soothsayer with her furtive head movements, hunched shoulders and black clothing from head to toe. Both she and Serena appeared a little shocked as they looked over at him. They tiptoed to the table and left his dinner.

"I do something for you?" Mama Rosario asked in her deep alto voice.

"No. Leave it there," Nelson answered. But after his long day of programming, he had no energy to do anything and didn't touch the vegetable soup.

He went over to his Recliner and lay down for about an hour. Uncle Ernesto returned to get his tray and said gesturing at the soup, "You didn't eat."

"Oh, take it. I'm not hungry today," he said forcing himself to sit erect.

Uncle Ernesto pulled over a ladder back chair and sat next to him. He took a chocolate bar out of his shirt pocket and slowly took off the gold embossed paper, breaking off a piece and giving it to Nelson. Nelson took the chocolate and put it into his mouth.

"This is the best chocolate in the world." Uncle Ernesto said with pride. The wrapper had Spanish wording.

"It's good," Nelson said.

Uncle Ernesto broke off another piece, "Good? It's smooth and creamy." He broke off another piece and gave it to Nelson. "Try another piece. It's made in Peru. My brother gets crates of food every day from Peru for his restaurant. So it is very fresh."

Nelson rolled the chocolate over his tongue to savor the smooth creaminess of the rich morsel. Slowly he ate the whole chocolate bar piece by piece as Uncle Ernesto fed it to him. Its velvety texture was comforting.

Uncle Ernesto patted him on the shoulder, "You have a good night, amigo," he said and left with the tray.

Nelson then dragged himself to the computer. He still couldn't get the idea of the squirrel on Mars out of his mind. It gave him hope something else was out there.

He decided to run his program another time, letting it step through each little piece of the photo inch by inch to see if anything was there. This might take time but he would stare at his computer all night if he had to.

* * *

"Well, how's the Whizkid, this morning?" Harvey Fox popped his head into Edith Bleary's room at the Black Hills Assisted Living Center in Rapid City, South Dakota. It was mid-morning and she was on her computer, surfing the Web. Harvey was short, thin and wiry compared to Edith, who carried her 85 years with the girth and stability of a Plains pioneer woman.

"You won't believe what I found on Mars," she said to Harvey.

"Eh, you found something on Mars right here in South Dakota?" He went over by the computer Edith's nephew installed for her. Although she was born in a South Dakota sod house, she wasn't afraid of modern technology. She had hitched up plows, worked the baler, the cultivator and survived more tornadoes than she could count. She wasn't about to let a teeny little computer scare her.

On her screen at least ten computer windows were opened, one of which was clearly a live photo of Mars.

"See, here, there's some kind of critter on Mars right there trying to get into the crater."

"Oh, yeh, I see. Isn't that something? And he gets in there, too. It looks like a salamander or eel to me."

"Yeh, or could be a prairie dog or a squirrel. Don't forget it's thousands of miles from Mars, so the picture will be fuzzy and hard to make out." Edith explained to him. "And the critters aren't going to be like on the prairie either. There's no grass there for one thing. Look how it crashes into the crater will you. I'm glad we don't have those things around here."

"Are you sure that's a picture of Mars?" Harvey asked. He peered closer to the screen.

"Yes, see right there it says "Mars." Right there in the middle of this whole thing. They call it the address."

"Oh, yeh. I see now. Well, that's why you're the Whizkid." He looked close to the screen again. "Why does it print those other letters above the pictures?

"Oh, don't get confused now. There're a lot of funny names on these windows but you learn to ignore them. My nephew told me all this stuff is connected." She waved her hand in front of the screen.

"O.K. I don't know anything about computers. It's too much for an old Black Hills gold miner like me."

"They're not so hard when you get to know them," Edith said.

Harvey leaned closer to the computer screen. "Is that Mars?" he asked again.

"It does look peculiar, don't it?"

He shrugged his shoulders and grinned. "I don't want to tell you what it looks like to me," he said with a wink.

"I don't want to hear, you old coot. I know the way you think. It's Sunday, you know. I want to see you at the church service this afternoon."

"O.K. I'll be there praying for my sins." Harvey chuckled and left her to her Web surfing.

51

* * *

"Whizkid, send me your E-Mail address. I'll give you mine. I have a few questions." Nelson typed his E-Mail into the Chat Room. He had not slept during the night, staring at the screen as though it were an oracle. After about ten minutes he got an E-Mail from EBleary. He sent her another E-Mail with specific instructions to get the address of the window she was looking at. After several E-Mails between them he got an address different from the original Mars window.

Nelson typed it in and began coughing vigorously as he saw a demo of a sperm piercing into the wall of an egg on a family planning site. The crater in the Mars photo did bear a resemblance to the circular egg in the demo, even the burnt sienna coloring was the same in both windows. He put his sunken cheeks into his two bony hands and began sobbing. It was ten o'clock on Sunday morning and he heard a knock on his door. He said, "Come in" but when Serena entered with his food he continued to sob, blowing his nose and coughing intermittently. Serena said, "Are you O.K., Mr. Mayfield?" He continued to cough and cry. Serena tried to hand him a tissue but he ignored her and she finally ran out of the room. He had no energy left. What was he thinking, looking for a squirrel on Mars? He laughed sardonically. He was not squirrel material in this life or an afterlife.

Several minutes later he could hear Serena, Mama Rosario, and Uncle Ernesto outside the door talking in hushed tones with each other. He tried to control his coughing, blow his nose and wipe his eyes and then said, "Come in." A few minutes passed while the whispering outside his door continued. Finally Uncle Ernesto entered carrying a scruffy portable tape deck. He went over to the CD player and pressed the power button off.

"Here's something to make you feel better," Uncle Ernesto

said. He pressed a few buttons on the tape deck and a Mariachi band played a lively Mexican song in Spanish.

Nelson turned and looked at Uncle Ernesto who was smiling broadly at him while swaying to the music. He came over and put his muscular arm around Nelson's thin shoulders. "This is better to listen to. Believe me."

Nelson felt a warm feeling go through his body from Uncle Ernesto's hug. He began to move gently to the Mariachi music along with Uncle Ernesto. Nelson turned to Uncle Ernesto and said softly, "Thank you." And then looking into his eyes added, "I do believe you."

I Stop for Falcons

"They're identifying birds, Jonathan. What a weird group. They feel compelled to identify each and every bird on the planet. Stay away from them. It may be catchy." I am bantering with my ten-year-old son as we pass by some birders while I drive from the Holiday Inn in Solomons Island in southern Maryland to the boat dock. I promised Jonathan a full day on the Chesapeake Bay while his mother is visiting her sister in Montreal. We like to spend long weekends at Solomons Island because it's only two hours from our home and the surrounding water brings back memories of our leisurely way of life in Barbados.

"What're they looking at, Dad? Can we stop and look through the big telescope?" my son asks stretching his seat-belt restraints to gaze out the side window at the birders.

"We cannot stop. We are late already—because you insisted on swimming in the hotel pool this morning. It's already quarter to nine and we have to meet on the Solomons dock at nine sharp."

It was my fault for allowing Jonathan to swim this morning but I tend to indulge my son who has had a hard life already with his allergies and eczema. When he was a baby, I took turns with my wife waking him up in the middle of the night to change the bandages and ointment we put over his whole body so that he would not itch himself to death. I've lost so much sleep over the years my eyes look permanently drowsy.

Jonathan fidgets with his sun hat. He turns it inside out, puts it back on his head then beams at me for my reaction.

"You're acting like a clown," I say. "Do you want to join the circus? You can tour the country with the Fat Lady, the Flying Wallendas and the freak show. Would you like that?"

"I'd like to fly in the air on a trapeze someday," he decides.

"I'll install a trapeze for you in the backyard over your mother's begonias so they can cushion your fall."

He smiles and says, "Are we there yet?" knowing I hate this.

"We are running late, Jonathan. That's why I don't like to wait until the last minute. We could have forgotten something." I look at our gym bag on the rear seat of the car. "Did you bring your wallet?"

"Got it." He slaps his pocket.

"Your sunscreen?"

"I think I left it at the pool."

"Left it at the pool! You want me to turn around and go back?" I say. My wife says I have a deep, deliberate way of speaking which commands respect.

"No, Dad. We'll miss the boat. I'll wear my long-sleeved shirt and my hat." He puts his hat on correctly. "My shirt's in the gym bag." He motions toward the back seat and rocks back and forth pleased with his solution.

"What else did you forget?" I ask "Your lunch? Your allergy medicine?" My son doesn't answer. "What, Jonathan, did you forget those, too?"

"I have my lunch but I think I forgot my allergy stuff," he says no longer smiling.

"You see what I mean when you hurry," I explain to him. "If your mother knew we forgot these things, she would wring both our necks." My wife says I'm a good father as long as she's around. I always tell her that's why I like to keep her around as much as possible.

"I'll be careful, Dad. I won't eat anything but my own lunch," Jonathan says. He's been trained since birth to eat only what we prepare at home for him and I'm satisfied he'll do this.

We pass the bridge that crosses the Patuxent River near the Chesapeake Bay.

"Is that not a beautiful engineering feat?" I say, hugging him. I want him to enjoy the day. "That's called a continuous span beam bridge. Look at the concrete piers that support it and how nicely it curves across the river." I was educated in engineering in Great Britain at one of the Queen's best colleges.

"Cool," my son says. "Are there big fish in the water? Do you think we'll see a whale or a shark?" he turns to me, his eyes widening.

"A whale! Whales are 50 or 60 feet. That's as long as four cars. I hope we don't see a whale or we might be in the belly of the whale," I laugh.

"Fifty feet. Is that bigger than the boat?" Jonathan asks.

"They're about the same size but the whale has teeth as big as your arm," I say. "I'm glad I'm an engineer and don't have to worry about such dangerous animals. Engineering is a nice, dependable living and if you're a good engineer, no one cares about the color of your skin, or what country you come from, or whether you hold your glasses together with adhesive tape."

Jonathan laughs, "That's a nerd, Dad."

"Please, do not say that word in my presence. We engineers are very sensitive about that. Tell me, what is Pi?"

"3.14159," he answers.

"Oh, I was thinking, apple," I say.

"Cherry," he says.

"Banana cream," I say. We keep this up for a few minutes.

Jonathan looks out the front windshield stretching his neck to see why the cars are slowing down. There's only one two-lane road leading into Solomons Island. On the left are shops and restaurants and on the right is a boardwalk along the Patuxent River.

"Now what is holding up traffic?" I complain. We start to move at a snail's pace and I see more birders standing in front of the line of cars. When I made the reservations, I didn't know a Birding Festival was scheduled at Solomons for the same weekend.

"They are right in the middle of the road. Look at them, Jonathan. If they raise their binoculars any higher, the birds will have a good shot at their half-opened mouths." We both roar at the prospect.

"They're looking at something on top of that telephone pole. See next to the Oyster House" Jonathan points to the house on the left.

"These, idiots. Why they are not moving?" I'm perturbed. "Holding up traffic like this, ignoring the rest of us. They don't even flinch when we pass by. We could run them right over. Imagine, risking their lives to look at a bird." I notice one of their parked cars has a bumper sticker saying "I Stop for Falcons."

"What bird?" Jonathan leans forward to see.

"I don't know what bird, any bird," I grumble. The stream of cars drive slowly past the birders and I roll my window down and shout at them, "You're making me miss my boat, Man. What's wrong with you standing in the middle of the road!" A few of them look at me perplexed; nothing registers with them but birds. If I shouted "pelican" or "eagle," then they might react.

We drive another mile and pull into the parking lot at the dock. I grab our Adidas gym bag and we both run to find the boat captain.

"Excuse me, Man. I'm Thomas and this is my son, Jonathan," I say to a wiry old black guy.

"Ike," he says shaking my hand.

"Did you see a boat this morning called "The Whaler"?"

"Took off five minutes ago," he stammers.

"I knew this would happen," I groan. "Our boat left, Jonathan. We missed it because of those birders." Jonathan sits down on the dock and pouts.

"What birders?" Ike asks. "Did you see the birders? I'm waiting on some birders to take them on a Pelagic bird trip in my boat." He points to a battered tour boat, named "The Catfish", a shabby vessel compared to The Whaler which I had sailed on before.

"What is a Pelagic bird trip?" I ask him.

"Take 'em out far enough to see birds that don't come to land. Like the shearwater bird. They like to see that. Maybe they'll let you come along."

Jonathan's expression implores me to go. I look at "The Catfish" with some misgivings.

"How much will it cost us to go with you?"

"If it's O.K. with the bird group, you can come along for $10 each." I couldn't argue with this price and decide to go. I can't disappoint my son who has been looking forward to this for many days. We wait with Ike for the birders. I roughhouse with Jonathan who is full of energy and anxious to be off.

"So you'll have your boat trip after all," I say, "And tomorrow we'll go to the nuclear power plant at Calvert Cliffs." He does not react. "There's a museum next to it that has Indian fossils," I say.

"Of animals?" he perks up.

"All kinds," I answer.

After twenty minutes of waiting, fifteen birders amble toward us in groups of two and three. Most of them are still searching the sky with their binoculars.

"Did you ever see such a strange group?" I say to Ike. We had become friendly, comparing notes on my upbringing in

Barbados and his childhood in Southern Maryland, a fisherman and boater since he was a boy.

"I seen a lot in my day," he laughs. "Nothin' surprises me no more." He heads over to the group.

"How ya doin' this mornin'?" he greets the birders. "Beautiful day for a boat trip. There's nice wind and I hear the fish are bitin'. That's always a good sign down here in Solomons."

"Hi, I'm Marsha from the Maryland Audubon Group." She bows, shifting her weight back and forth. "I think I went on a boat passage with you on the Chesapeake Bay before."

Ike looks confused but answers, "Oh, yeh, O.K.," he says. "I'm Ike."

Marsha has short gray hair and is probably in her fifties but it's hard to tell because she's thin like a jogger and seems very energetic. The other birders gather around her like a bunch of old hens with an occasional old rooster, probably in need of some Viagra, I laugh to myself. They are encumbered with backpacks, fanny packs, shoulder bags and pouches on their canvas vests, all filled to the hilt. Several carry scopes on tripods and all have binoculars slung around their necks. They must be anticipating a tidal wave or tsunami on this trip, I chuckle quietly. They're a credit to emergency preparedness.

"Everyone, this is Ike. He'll be our captain today on the "The Catfish," Marsha bellows, her arms moving about expressively as she talks.

"Mind if I take these two with me?" Ike asks Marsha. "They missed "The Whaler" this mornin' and the man promised the little fella a ride in a boat."

"Sure, that's O.K. with me," Marsha answers.

"Thank you," I say. "I was delayed by some birders in the middle of the highway, no doubt searching the air for some rare bird."

"And you are right. We saw a falcon, either a kestrel or a

peregrine falcon; we aren't quite sure. When we aren't sure, we call it a 'falcon, species unknown'," she says.

"It was a peregrine," the old rooster says, "He was standing sentry up on the pole like peregrines do. They're brave birds. They can dive-bomb after their prey at 200 miles per hour."

"No, it was a kestrel. It had a reddish back," an elderly woman argues. She holds a bird book two inches from her eyes examining pictures of various birds.

The group shuffles around still searching the air with their binoculars, some looking to the east, some to the west, some to the north, while Marsha rambles on about their boat trip. Standing back and observing them, I think they're all "species unknown." What a sorry prospect to be spending a full day with them on this boat. But it will make my son happy.

"I'm sorry if we held you up," Marsha says to me. "You can certainly join us on our trip. And maybe we can even point out some natural wonders to you and your son."

"Oh, you don't have to do that. I only promised Jonathan a ride on the high seas," I say. "We are from Barbados and we love the water."

"How long have you been in this country?" she asks.

"I'm here fifteen years so we are well-indoctrinated in American ways."

"Well, glad to have you along and let's go around and introduce ourselves again. The whole group including myself and Jonathan are forced into this social ritual of describing ourselves in one sentence.

After the last birder expresses her interest in seeing a pelican, I say, "I'm Thomas. I'm an engineer for a cell phone company in Baltimore and this is my son, Jonathan." Jonathan says, "I'm Jonathan. I'm in the 5th grade at Baltimore Prep Middle School. I want to see a shark on the trip." I'm proud of my son who is a very mature and polished speaker for his age.

"I don't know if we'll see everything everyone wants to see," Marsha says, "but I think we'll see some shearwaters, petrels, and pelicans and, Jonathan, I think we may even see a shark or two.

"I can't wait," Jonathan jumps around excited about our prospects.

"Hopefully, it won't be a Great White Shark, Jonathan. We don't want too much excitement," Marsha says.

No, we don't want anyone's pacemaker to give out on the high seas, I laugh to myself.

We all board "The Catfish" and Ike gets the craft underway. I stick with him and his assistant, Woody, at the boat controls. We are all black and I still feel more comfortable with them even though my education is probably nearer to the birders.

"Ten dollars each," Ike says.

"Oh, I forgot. Business is business," I laugh giving him a twenty dollar bill.

"Could I go over with them, Dad?" Jonathan pleads pointing to the birders.

"O.K." I say, "But do not stand on the benches to look over the side." He scampers to the other end of the boat and inserts himself in the middle of the group to listen to Marsha who is talking enthusiastically about the air, the sea, the birds and the fish. I look at Ike and we both chuckle.

"Talkin' a mean streak," he says.

Woody chimes in, "Yak, Yak, Yak, Yak."

"Hey, Man, did you ever meet a woman who couldn't talk non-stop once she gets started?" I say.

"That's the truth," Ike says. "They can't seem to just be."

We go out to sea, comfortable companions, saying a word here or there. The rhythmic lapping of the waves reminds me of my childhood home in Barbados which I left at eighteen but still visit once a year. We pass Drum Point and head into the waters of the Chesapeake Bay.

I occasionally look over to see if Jonathan is all right. The birders have adopted him, providing him with a pair of small binoculars and endless information on the birds flying overhead. He points in the sky and asks, "What's that?" every ten seconds. I'm amused at my good fortune in enlisting the birders as my babysitters.

Marsha gathers the birders and my son around her to examine some seaweed-like matter she has mysteriously produced. Jonathan picks it up in turn and taunts one of his birder buddies with the seaweed. It makes me flinch. I don't like him handling strange substances because of his eczema and allergies.

"Jonathan. Jonathan. Put that down," I say. I go over to him with an antibacterial packet. "Here, let me wash your hands." I clean him off as best I can and say to the group, "Do not give him anything to touch. He has allergies." I look at him crossly and he turns away. "You know better, Jonathan," I say. I stay with him for ten minutes and he appears to be O.K. so I gravitate back to Ike maneuvering past these ancient mariners, wondering how many hours these old relics have spent in the sun. I will be seeing old age spots in my sleep tonight.

Ike has picked up speed and we are now well away from land with vast expanses of water all around us like in the Caribbean. I imagine that the water is green like in Barbados and that the blowing marsh reeds on the distant shores are the curved fronds of palm trees. Twenty minutes go by. I hear Jonathan laughing with his new friends in the background.

"What's that ahead of us," I ask Ike as I see a spot on the horizon.

"Just a waterman, probably crabbin'. We're in the Chesapeake Bay now. Great crabbin' out here. We're headin' for the Chesapeake Bay Bridge Tunnel near Norfolk to see the pelagic birds there.

"I love crabs," I say, "but my son is allergic, so I never go to crab restaurants with him."

The boat gets closer and Ike and the other captain signal each other. I notice "The Catfish's" communications gear is rudimentary for the times. Within ten minutes, the other boat which is filled with crabs approaches and the fishy odor reeks over to "The Catfish." The smell makes me feel good to be on the seas again with men who are the salt of the earth. The crab boat is so close I shout over to the captain, "Did you get a good catch?"

He hollers back, "Pretty good. Can't complain."

"Maybe I'll be eating some of those in a restaurant tonight," I yell to him.

"Guaranteed fresh," he says and we banter some more before he passes by.

When I turn around to the birders, I'm alarmed to see Marsha kneeling down holding Jonathan who has collapsed. I rush over knocking into objects on the boat and a few of the birders. I kneel down and pull Jonathan away from Marsha and take him in my arms. He's gasping for breath and I recognize that he's having a delayed allergic reaction. I admonish myself for not staying with him after he touched the seaweed.

"Does anyone have an Epi-Pen or allergy medicine?" I ask, my voice elevated above the sound of the boat's motor. There's no response and I see Ike turn his back to me and busy himself with the boat controls.

"I believe I have a homeopathic remedy," Marsha shouts searching in her over-stuffed backpack across the way.

"No, I mean Chlor-Trimeton or Claritin, anything." I say. There's no answer.

"In all those backpacks, there's not one pill for allergies?"

I shout at the group and see only those same perplexed expressions I observed earlier when I yelled at them to move off the road.

Marsha approaches swiftly while I sit back on my heels holding Jonathan's head in my lap. "Ike is turning the boat back to shore," she says as she dives toward Jonathan and puts something in his mouth with an eyedropper before I can stop her.

"Do not touch my son," I scream at her. "You are responsible for this, giving him that seaweed to hold. And now you think you can magically make this go away with some old wives' potion."

Marsha looks at me as though I'm mad. "Are you happy now to witness my son's death?" I cry to all of them. I thrash my arms about in despair convinced that my son is gone from me. Marsha lays Jonathan down flat on the deck and elevates his legs on her bulging backpack. She begins administering mouth-to-mouth to my boy. I must allow her to do this because I've never been able to master the technique, although my wife is proficient at it. I think with grief how I will tell her what I have done to our son. Kneeling by him, I touch his shoulder. He's breathing very faintly now and I don't take my eyes from him lest he stop breathing completely.

After many minutes, the murmuring of the birders in the background turns to shouting. I see a Coast Guard boat coming toward us and I get up and yell out repeatedly. "My son's having an allergic attack." They close in on "The Catfish" and one of them quickly boards the boat and rushes in with medical equipment. He pulls out an Epi-Pen and plunges it into Jonathan's thigh. In only a few minutes my son begins to breathe better. The Coast Guard transfers Jonathan to their vessel with great skill and authority. I'm allowed to go with them and think "good riddance" to these birders who have almost cost me the life of my son with their acute and ridiculous examination of nature.

Jonathan is reviving and I'm becoming more relieved as I hold his hand and wipe his face, kissing him gently on the brow.

The Coast Guard boat is much faster than "The Catfish" and we arrive on shore in twenty minutes. A police car and an ambulance are waiting at the dock to take us to the Solomons Urgent Care Center. By now Jonathan has become more responsive and I feel a large weight lift from me.

When we get to the medical center, Jonathan is attended by several doctors, nurses, and ambulance and police personnel in the emergency area. I'm allowed to stand aside the gurney as he regains his liveliness. I stroke his arms and forehead and think my son is still with me. How grateful I am.

The doctors seem satisfied that Jonathan has stabilized and one of them comes over to me and says, "He's a lucky boy. The pseudoephedrine and mouth-to mouth probably bought enough time to save him."

"He was given pseudoephedrine?" I ask.

"Yes, the bottle that was brought in by the Coast Guard." He holds up the vial that Marsha administered. "It's a stimulant."

I did not know what Jonathan was given, but I'm now feeling guilty about my conduct to Marsha who may have saved the life of my boy, although, I remind myself, she may have also put him in jeopardy with the seaweed he was handling.

"My son was touching seaweed just before the attack," I tell the doctor, "Could that have caused it?"

"No, Dad, it was the smell of the crabs on the boat that passed by us," my son interjects.

"Yes, it's the shellfish," the Doctor says jiggling Jonathan's allergy bracelet. "I see this all the time down here. Pronounced smells from shellfish can set off a shellfish allergy in sensitive people."

I feel a surge of shame. I have accused Marsha of injuring my son with the seaweed and it was I who was cajoling with the watermen on the trawler causing them to linger in the area. The burden of my transgressions weigh on me as my son becomes more spirited.

"He'll have to stay here for a few hours until he stabilizes completely. Take him to your allergist when you get home and have a blood test done to see just how allergic he is to shellfish," the doctor says.

"We were lucky the Coast Guard was in the vicinity," I say to the Doctor.

"I understand someone from the Audubon Group called 9-1-1 on their cell phone," he answers. "The Solomons' Police Department patched them to the Coast Guard Rescue Center."

"I didn't know that," I murmur.

"He had one of those GPS Systems and kept relaying the position of your boat to the Coast Guard," the Doctor continues. "I was just talking about it over there with the Police. Amazing what you can do these days with over-the-counter equipment."

I don't tell him I know exactly how this works because I'm an engineer in the mobile phone business. I feel ashamed that I was not prepared and resourceful enough to have done the same for my son.

I try to amuse Jonathan but I feel so guilty about my behavior I can't rejoice in his recovery as I should. We are released from the hospital by evening and go back to the motel in Solomons. I stay by his side all night and hardly sleep.

* * *

The next day I set out with Jonathan to see if I can find the birding group to thank them for saving the life of my son and to apologize for my behavior. I stop at the Marsh Walk at the Calvert Marine Museum where many birders are identifying birds in the creek, but I don't see Marsha or anyone from the trip. I search among the birders like the birders search for birds looking for identifiable marks: short grey hair, large green back-pack, very energetic behavior. If I don't find what I'm looking for at one site, I migrate to another site in search of the species I now feel compelled to find.

Jonathan and I get in the car and drive slowly through the streets of Solomons. From time to time I put my arm around his shoulders and pat his hand. I stop at the Chesapeake Biological Lab at the southernmost point of Solomons where some more birders have congregated.

"Do you see that antenna, Jonathan," I say. He nods. "It's the GPS system that saved your life yesterday." He ignores what I say trying to forget his ordeal.

"What about the fossils? I thought we were going to see the fossils today?" he says.

"I want to find Marsha first and the other birders to thank them for helping you," I say.

"I have an idea," he exclaims, "Why don't we send them a "Thank You" card."

I stop and look at my son who rocks back and forth delighted at his own suggestion. "You are so wise, Jonathan. That is exactly what we will do." I pledge to find the address of the Maryland Audubon Group when I get home and send them a note of thanks for all they did for me and my boy.

We approach a birder with short grey hair, the same species as Marsha, I think.

"What is it you're looking at?" I ask.

"A peregrine falcon," she replies. "Would you like to see it in the scope?"

"I've been told they're worth stopping traffic for," I say moving slowly toward the scope. I look through the beautiful optical device focusing on the falcon and admire the clarity of the lens as it brings the majestic bird into view while my heart feels relieved and hopeful.

Jubilant Voices

Nathanael Early filled his lungs to their maximum capacity, before he sang the rousing "Glory, Glory Hallelujah ..." of "The Battle Hymn of the Republic." Even with perfect technique, he could not match the volume and grandeur of the new tenor's tone.

He felt he was at a disadvantage being five foot four and 107 pounds and that was during the winter. In the summer when he perspired heavily, he fought daily to keep his weight over 100 pounds. He had come to terms with his physical deficiencies by making prudent choices to minimize his deformities, for his weight was not the worst of it. He had a peculiarly-shaped head. His forehead and chin both slanted sharply back making his head look too small for his emaciated frame like a shrunken head in an anthropology exhibit. He was rather pleased when his hairline began to recede and his forehead appeared broader.

His one point of pride since he was a youth was his rich tenor voice. When he was singing, his distorted physical appearance would recede into the background and everyone would focus on his lyrical voice. He perfected his technique through years of lessons and now at age 52 was lead tenor in The Jubilant Voices of Culpeper choral society; that is, he was lead tenor until Trudy Stemple moved to the Virginia countryside from New York to be near her son. The choral director decided that Trudy's voice was better suited to the tenor range and register and since there was a dearth of good tenors, she was added to the tenor ranks.

"Haven't I bolstered the tenors for years?" he reasoned with the Director.

"You've done more than your share, Nathanael. But what if you are ill one day? You know the remaining tenors have no volume. You <u>are</u> the tenor section but I don't want to put you under such pressure." And so Trudy became the seventh tenor.

To further infuriate him, at six feet and 200 pounds, Trudy was twice his size. He had to stand adjacent to her in the choral group and endure the humiliation of hundreds of eyes from the audience looking at them with amusement. The universe was mocking him. His mind wandered to his distant relative from the Civil War, General Jubal Early, who lost a number of battles in the Shenandoah Valley nearby Culpeper. He shuddered—what humiliation the Earlys have had to endure.

Trudy seemed oblivious to the affront she had visited on him. She was very self-absorbed, continually blowing her nose from her all-season allergies, polishing her black-rimmed glasses, fidgeting with strands of hair, tucking in her clothes. She wore garish, flowery blouses and tight-fitting skirts emphasizing her melon-like abdomen. She also used a floral scent that Nathanael could barely endure but was forced to breathe in for hours while they practiced or performed.

Nathanael never considered himself unkind, but since this New Yorker trudged into his life, he found he was not as peaceful as he thought. He was growing increasingly hostile to Trudy. When she first joined The Jubilant Voices he had a very interesting conversation with her about Gluck's *Alceste* and was quite impressed with her musicology. But that was before he found out she was singing tenor. Already she performed a tenor solo he would ordinarily have sung.

"Nathanael!" The choral director was trying to get his attention for some time.

"Yes?" Nathanael responded.

"Please take it from measure 32 with the upbeat."

Nathanael concentrated on his breathing technique and then began singing "In the beauty of the lilies Christ was born across the sea ..." His tone was so delicate, so refined, it would have made Placido Domingo take notice. As he was coming to the most poignant verse, he heard a cell phone ring. Trudy rustled through her tote bag and finally silenced the disagreeable buzzing. Nathanael stopped abruptly.

"I can't sing if she's going to be interrupting all the time."

Trudy looked over, chagrined. "Oh, sorry. I would turn it off during a performance."

"Well, I hope so," he said angrily.

The choral director was annoyed. "C'mon. C'mon now. We don't have all day. Trudy you take it now from 'In the beauty of the lilies.'"

"Sure," she said tugging at her bra strap underneath her blouse. The pianist played the introduction and Trudy got her clothes adjusted just in time to begin the hymn.

She had a full, sonorous voice that no one could ignore. The whole chorus, including the director, looked on in amazement. Nathanael himself had his mouth slightly opened as he stared at her. Suddenly he became panicky. He could see where this was going. She would get "The Battle Hymn of the Republic" too. It was not enough that she got to sing the "Ave Maria" last month.

Nathanael fumbled in his pocket for his handkerchief. He needed a diversionary tactic fast. He began coughing as loud as he could but it didn't make a dent in the sound coming from her mighty lungs that had expanded her chest to look like Brunnhilde. When she completed the solo verse, the chorus broke into applause. She glanced briefly at Nathanael and smiled self-consciously, "Thanks ... Thanks."

"Very nice, Trudy," the choral director said, "O.K. everyone, final practice tomorrow at seven. Be on time."

This was too much. Nathanael's world was disintegrating.

When Nathanael got home, he went down to his basement to work on the miniature Civil War battlefields he had been constructing for the last seventeen years. He taught history at the 5th grade level, a choice calculated around his size. He was fairly confident he would be the largest one in the room except for an aberration here or there, like the Utley twins, who were held back two years in a row. But they were as lethargic as his hounddog, Beauregard, and he didn't see any problem there.

At least 75% of his basement was now battlefield with Gettysburg dominating. He scooted his stool over to Little Roundtop and moved the two-inch Union soldiers away from the action as though they were fleeing the Southern forces who now charged toward Little Roundtrop attempting to take the hill.

Then he went over by the battles of the Shenandoah Valley where General Jubal Early suffered overwhelming defeats for the South. He placed both hands on the edge of the display and bent over to survey the Shenandoah battlefield. Sometimes he would contrive different strategies for the South to win critical battles in the Shenandoah Valley and he had become quite an expert on those battles having written a paper describing how the General might have evaded defeat. He had presented the paper to an audience of five at the annual Gettysburg book festival and was wildly applauded by one of the Southern spectators with whom he still corresponded. He shook his head back and forth and sighed.

Well, enough of this procrastinating, he thought. He rolled up his sleeves. He performed maintenance work on the

Burnside Bridge in the Antietam exhibit with his hot glue gun and then went over to the platform behind the furnace. Last week he cleaned out storage boxes to make space to construct the Battle of Vicksburg. He planned to build the fortress-like bluffs along the Mississippi near Vicksburg that played such a big role in Vicksburg's defense. He had even thought about constructing the mighty Mississippi with real water but that would be tricky.

"Nathanael, where are you? Oh, where have you gone?" He heard his mother calling from the upstairs.

"Down here, Mother. His dog, Beauregard, was supposed to be guarding the front entrance but lately he seemed to spend twenty hours a day sleeping. Culpeper was a neighborly town but he expected Beauregard to warn him of visitors.

His mother came clunking down the steps with her high heels. She was about the same size as Nathanael except that her miniature head was covered by a mound of teased platinum hair, sculpted back from her face, which made her head look too big for her body.

"Oh, Nathanael, still with the little soldiers at your age."

"It's for my students, Mother. Young people need to be stimulated visually to grasp history." Nathanael was vexed at his mother's misrepresentation of his hobby.

"But there's no place to walk down here anymore."

"There are aisles here," he pointed out.

"If your father were alive to see what he started with the tiny trains at Christmas."

"Mother, you know I'm in the National Guard. This helps me focus on maneuvers. Let's go upstairs." He had never met a woman yet who understood the Civil War and its impact on the men of Virginia. Women never had to go to war. That was the difference. His father had collected Civil War artifacts and would approve of the battle exhibit. At his own request he was buried with an antique Confederate Officer's Sword that Nathanael liked to swish around from time to time. But it was an honor to grant his father's last wish and he created a little ceremony at the funeral whereby he placed the sword in the casket with a bow and a salute.

Nathanael escorted his mother upstairs and down the darkened hall with its brown wainscoting to the front foyer. A picture of General Early hung prominently in the foyer adjacent to a gilded mirror; the General's visage was the first thing seen when entering the house.

"Don't you remember when Father bought this Confederate spittoon at an estate sale in Middleburg, Mother." He pointed to the tarnished object on the floor just under General Early's picture.

"Oh, don't remind me. You and your father. The money in these souvenirs," she said.

"It's history, Mother—our history."

"Yes. Yes, Nathanael. I am very proud of you," she said patting his arm. "What I wanted to tell you is I've taken a notion to bake a cake or a pie for your solo performance next week. All my lady friends will be there and I think pastry at intermission will suit the occasion since it's in the afternoon."

"I don't know if I'll sing the solo this time, Mother. I have competition now."

"Nonsense, Nathanael. Your voice is as sweet as a hermit thrush singing in a Magnolia tree. You are the heart and soul of Jubilant Voices."

"Thank you, Mother, for your vote of confidence but there are a number of excellent voices in the choral group."

"What other voices? Let me just have a talk with Harry Stephens and we'll see who sings the solo. You know, I got him appointed as the board president of Jubilant Voices."

"Mother, there's no need to interfere. I'm sure I'll sing

the solo." But he wasn't now. There was a good chance Trudy would get it.

"Interfere. Was it interfering when I worked all those summer days to raise money for the group? All those antique sales I organized, selling items from your father's old Civil War paraphernalia and then the bake sale, all those key lime pies I made."

"You did more than anyone, Mother. And we appreciate it." But he never forgave his mother for selling his father's Civil War memorabilia. Women had no sense of history.

"And don't forget who named the group, Jubilant Voices," she said.

No, he would never forget. Every time he heard someone in the chorus joking about the name, he cringed with the secret knowledge of his mother's culpability.

"How about if I make lemon squares for a light refreshment?"

"That would be lovely, Mother." He guided his mother to the door trying to get rid of at least one problem.

Nathanael opened the door and almost pushed her out. "Goodbye, Mother. Please don't concern yourself. I'm sure I'll be singing solo."

He breathed a sigh of relief and then alternately gazed at the picture of General Early and the adjacent mirror. Perhaps, around the eyes, he mused.

At rehearsal the next evening, the choral director pulled Nathanael aside, "I'm going to give you a break this year and have Trudy sing the solo just for a change. See how it works with a woman's voice. You can relax a little."

Nathanael flushed but he quickly recovered. "Good. I won't have to medicate myself this year." He looked over toward Trudy who was looking at him and the director. She knew what they were talking about, he was sure.

"O.K., everyone. Take your places," the director shouted.

Nathanael dragged himself to his spot next to Trudy who

was even now pulling in her nose and searching for a Kleenex. She seemed completely oblivious to his grief. How could he get through this? He couldn't even tell his mother. He feared she would mobilize her volunteer forces and start something with the Board.

The Director waved his baton to start the rehearsal of "The Battle Hymn of the Republic." He loved this song. Both the North and South sang their own versions during the Civil War but to him it now evoked the anguish, unfairness and valor Southerners experienced. Surely he could put deeper feeling into this memorable hymn than Trudy who was from the North—the North, which seemed to have shrugged off the Civil War a long time ago. Her voice was brilliant, true, but where was the pathos?

Trudy suddenly stopped singing and was fumbling in her purse for something. "What's wrong?" The choral director was annoyed.

"I can't find my glasses," she said searching through her purse. "I can't read the music without them."

"You can't see at all?" he asked.

"I really need them," she said, "Oh, here they are."

The choral director looked upset but resumed the piece and Trudy's singing was so powerful he seemed to forget about the episode. Nathanael could not believe she was going to get away with this. It was a disgrace to be so unprepared at rehearsal. He knew all the verses by heart and barely even looked at the music.

In the week leading up to The Jubilant Voices' performance, Nathanael relaxed with his hobby in the basement. He had already started building the Vicksburg terrain with corrugated cardboard and chicken wire. He put on a plastic apron as he prepared to cover the base with the paper mache to form the Mississippi river bluffs. He crushed the mound at different points to make the riverbank look realistic. With each crushing motion, he could feel his anger with Trudy Stemple. When he thought about General Grant winning at Vicksburg, the image of Trudy Stemple in a Yankee General's uniform popped into his head. He usually was so calm and peaceful while constructing these little battles but here he was thinking about Trudy Stemple.

The day of the grand performance Nathanael had finally admitted defeat. His mother was sitting in the audience with her lady friends waiting for his solo in "The Battle Hymn of the Republic." He was lying to her all week about singing it. At least this had temporarily stopped her from confronting the choral board. He was thinking of what he should tell her. Perhaps he could say he came down with a bit of laryngitis or a sore throat and wouldn't be at his best. What lame excuses. Why not just say his dog, Beauregard, ate his music like his fifth graders would.

The choral director motioned to start "The Battle Hymn of the Republic." Trudy Stemple began turning pages looking for the song, pulling in her nose and pushing on her glasses which popped off and fell between Nathanael's two feet. He could see them on the floor quite clearly but they were blocked from everyone else's view. Trudy was turned in the opposite direction. The organ was now resounding with the introduction to "The Battle Hymn." In a split second he crushed the glasses into the ground with his shoe. He looked down at them and wondered how he could have done such a thing? He quickly stooped to get them and handed the broken glasses to Trudy who looked alarmed. "You'll have to sing," she whispered to Nathanael.

"Fine," he quietly responded and the singing started.

When they got to the solo section the Director was surprised but adapted quickly to the change. Nathanael was never in better voice and the audience applauded enthusiastically at the end of the piece. He felt jubilant and vindicated by the rousing reception.

"How wonderful!" his mother's lady friends greeted him afterwards. "What a marvelous voice you have! And what feeling!"

Once he was home, Nathanael went down to his basement to savor his choral success while working on the Battle of Vicksburg. He hummed "The Battle Hymn of the Republic." Focused on his soldiers he heard someone rapping at the open screen door. Where was Beauregard? "Who's there?" he shouted.

"It's Trudy Stemple."

Nathanael was perplexed. Trudy visited his home once to pick up music, the time they discussed Gluck. "Come in. I'm down in the basement," he yelled. Soon the 200-pound body was slowly descending the open-backed stairs pausing after each step.

"Oh! What is this?" she exclaimed beholding the Civil War extravaganza.

"It's for the kids. You know I'm a history teacher. I've created mockups of several Civil War battles in my basement and once a year I bring the best students here for a history lesson."

"It's magnificent," she gushed holding one plump hand against her cheek in amazement. "It's breathtaking." She began wandering around the basement looking at various sections.

"Gettysburg," she said. "What a hallowed spot. You could sense the importance of the place."

"Yes," Nathanael said.

"And this must be Antietam. I've visited there so often I can tell it right off. That's the Burnside Bridge, isn't it?" He nodded.

"How lovely! Did you use match sticks for the bridge?"

"Oh, yes, I practically buy them by the crate."

"Oh. And you've built the whole Shenandoah Valley. It looks so idyllic. How wonderful!" She was bending over to look closely at the figurines of the soldiers. Oh, Nathanael, how talented you are, not only in singing but in history and theatrics!"

She waved her hand across the series of miniature battles.

Nathanael was speechless. It was a curious reaction for a New Yorker and a woman, too. His fifth graders would get excited when they first viewed the display and he would get a lot of "Awesomes" from the boys. But Trudy seemed genuinely impressed. He began to feel a twinge of guilt about stepping on her glasses. She must have had another pair stashed someplace because she was wearing them now.

"I just came by to thank you for filling in for me this afternoon," she said.

"No bother," he shrugged, "I've sung it a million times."

"And wonderfully, too, wonderfully," she replied. I could see how it must be a favorite of yours with your Civil War interests."

"Yes, you know, I'm a distant relative to General Jubal Early."

"Was that his picture in the hall? I could see the resemblance now that you mention it."

Imagine. Trudy thinks he looks like Jubal Early. Another pang of guilt came over him.

"Well, I don't want to keep you from your work," she said.

They stared at each other smiling for a moment.

"I have to go," Trudy said, "I just wanted to thank you for bailing me out. Clumsy me."

"Not at all," he said calmly.

Trudy turned to go and he began singing "The Battle Hymn of the Republic" in a soft voice. As she was ascending the stairs she turned to look at him and smiled. She joined in singing with him as she was leaving and it was only after she had gone out the front door that he realized they were both singing the solo part, the part she did not know by heart.

A Year in Beverly Hills

"My mother lived here in 1938 when she was twenty," Julie said to the woman at the outdoor cafe on Beverly Drive. They had chatted at the same coffee shop the day before.

"Those were glamorous times here in Hollywood," the woman mused. She looked like a gracefully aging movie star from the 30's. Her hair was laced with platinum and she was wearing a tiny white Valentino jacket.

Julie was a youthful 55. She was celebrating her retirement with this trip to Beverly Hills. She helped the older woman who was struggling to untangle her poodle's leash which was wound around the wrought iron table.

"Thank you," the woman nodded. "I'm Myrna."

"Julie," she said in return. A few awkward seconds passed as both women sipped their coffee. "My mother often lamented that my grandmother would get pneumonia in the winter after washing her long hair because she was unable to get it dry. There were no hairdryers then and Pennsylvania winters are bitterly cold. And then my mother would become wistful about how she dried her hair outside in the sun the year she lived in Beverly Hills."

"Pneumonia. I'm making a mental note to get another hair dryer," Myrna said shaking her head.

Since the death of Julie's mother the previous summer, visions of her at different ages began creeping to the surface of her mind until the pervading image was her mother at twenty, an age that Julie knew only from photos and her own visualizations from her mother's glowing stories about her year in Beverly Hills. As a child she yearned with her mother for this world of sun, elegance, riches and pleasure and heralded her mother's youthful beauty to her playmates believing they were only a step removed from Hollywood royalty.

"Pennsylvania to Beverly Hills: that was a long drive in the 30's. Why did she come?" Myrna asked.

Her boss, Mr. Nathanson, moved to California with his family and took my mother with them," Julie said. "She was a personal secretary, babysitter, and jack-of-all-trades for him and his family. Mr. Nathanson was from Wilkes-Barre and owned a bus line.

"A Girl Friday," Myrna said blowing a long breath of smoke toward the grey sky which was slowly turning blue.

"Apparently," Julie answered, "but she was very fond of the family she worked for. We received photos from them every Christmas and my mother would become very cheerful." She thought of the other times when her mother was depressed, worrying about money mostly; her Dad, working irregular hours in the machine shop, had a hard time supporting his brood of six. When he came home from the plant, he was so tired he would lie on the living room floor and fall asleep while she did her homework next to his snoring body. Her mother was left to dole out the meager pay to the local merchants and the threatening utility companies.

"Every Christmas we'd get photos of the Nathanson's and their kids. My mother would rattle off their names as though I knew them. It made my mother so happy; California became my dream too. Have you ever heard of them?" Julie asked.

"Nathanson? No. Doesn't sound familiar," Myrna said.

"Maybe Sid, my husband, knows them. He's better at remembering names than me."

"I often wonder why someone as beautiful as my mother would leave a place like this." The sky was bright blue now and Julie breathed in the warm air feeling almost perfect sitting there conversing with this obliging stranger.

"Why did she go back to Pennsylvania?" Myrna asked.

"To marry my father, I think, but I was too young to dig deeper. And then it became past history. Lately though I've begun to wonder about it," Julie said.

"So you're curious about the place," Myrna said.

"I think of my mother in that era. She had perfect features and flawless skin like Ann Blyth or Jean Simmons in those airbrushed photos. The type of face you'd think would be discovered here in Beverly Hills."

"Getting discovered is easier and harder than you think. It depends on who is the discoverer, "Myrna said with a wave of her arm. "Did your mother die recently?" she asked.

"She died a year ago last June in 2000—twenty years after my Dad who was ten years older than her. Yesterday I walked around her old neighborhood near Gregory and Bedford. It's such a lovely neighborhood. I could see why she always went into these reveries about it."

"Had she stayed here we would have been neighbors," Myrna smiled. "My husband lived in our house all his life. It's a nice neighborhood. We could never afford to buy here now."

Sitting in the outside cafe, Julie perused the mission-style houses and exotic foliage on the next block. The terra cotta tiles on the roofs and the stucco walls, half-hidden by olive trees, blue-green palms and chartreuse citrus trees, stirred up the romanticism of her mother's lifelong longings for California. The sidewalks and tree lawns created an old-fashioned air of a thirties neighborhood.

"She told me she once saw Ronald Coleman walking by himself on Wilshire Boulevard just a few blocks from where she lived. And a few times she saw Loretta Young at Mass on Sunday at the Catholic Church she attended."

"It's beautiful here. I can't complain now that the last of my kids finally moved out of the house," Myrna said. "So what's on your program today?" She started to clean up the mess of napkins and Sweet-and-Low packets on the table and got up to go.

"I'd like to catch a glimpse of a real live movie star. I don't care which one, just something to put in my trip report when I get back. What would you suggest?"

"Try the Farmers Market. A number of stars shop there and you can pick up some good souvenirs," Myrna said.

"Good idea. I had that on my list," Julie said as they parted.

* * *

Julie strolled around the open air L.A. Farmers Market. At a Mexican craft table she purchased a metallic picture frame and at a Native American jewelry store she bought an opal ring similar to her mother's. She stopped at a Peruvian stall and perused a beautiful leather chest embossed with an intricate design.

"Half price," the saleswoman said, "$400."

"It's beautiful but I wouldn't be able to carry it on the plane," Julie said. It was over a cubic foot.

"We can ship it," the saleswoman said.

"It's beautiful but still too expensive and I really have no use for it." Julie walked on to the next stall, but the shopping was now beginning to overwhelm her and she was afraid she might purchase an armoire or something, now that she knew they would ship items.

She headed directly to the fried calamari for some lunch. This is what she really wanted and it wouldn't break the bank. Calamari and maybe later a pound of the "best fudge in the world" to go she mused. She could eat this sliver by sliver in her hotel room. After all she was on vacation.

The next morning Julie sat outside at The Coffee Bean Cafe bundled in her sweater drinking a cappuccino. Even in August Beverly Hills is sixty degrees at 9 a.m. and the skies are still grey from the smog. She wondered if there was smog in 1938. On summer mornings, Pennsylvania skies are deep blue and at nine it's already warm.

"Hello again." Myrna strode over to the cafe table.

"Hi, do you come here every morning?" Julie asked.

"Yes, I do. My husband swims in our pool and I take Ginger for a walk and then stop here," she said tying Ginger to an outside table before going into the cafe.

Julie shivered to think of swimming in this temperature but she noticed a few breaks in the grey smog. By 10 a.m. the sky would be deep blue like California should be, she thought.

"Did you go to the Farmers Market?" Myrna asked as she strolled out of the shop and placed her cup of coffee on the table next to Julie's.

"Yes. I loved it. I had fried calamari and bought a tub of fudge for the room," Julie laughed.

"What a combination! I'll have to try that for my bridge club," Myrna said.

"I milled around for hours. See the opal ring I bought. I loved all the variety of food and crafts. Mangoes, kiwis, Portuguese sausage, Cajun barbeque and caramel apples—and the international crafts!" Julie said.

"Lovely opal," Myrna said examining it.

"I also took some pictures in my mother's old neighborhood yesterday and was amazed at the variety of plants and trees. I saw a tree full of lemons and one with avocados. It's so convenient to have a supply of lemons in your backyard."

"There're a lot of beautiful yards around here," Myrna said.

"If you like, we can walk back to my home on Roxbury and you can see the pool and grounds. It's not far from here."

"I'd love that," Julie said. What an opportunity, she thought, to see one of the houses in her mother's old neighborhood.

Eventually Ginger was unleashed from the cafe table and the two women and poodle ambled down Gregory Way until they came to Roxbury. Myrna led Julie to her beige stucco house with its arched doorway and its Mexican-styled portico which was in-laid with splashes of navy, turquoise and yellow tile. The draping fronds of a palm tree curved over the corners of the house.

Myrna was taking care of her dog Ginger and left Julie in the living room. She noticed that the living room was very for-mal with antique gold wall-molding on cream walls. At the far end of the room, ornate wall sconces were hung on either side of the fireplace. Flowered drapes and lace panel curtains deco-rated the French doors. Myrna returned and opened the doors to access a charming outside space dominated by a curved pool with glistening aquamarine water, stone pathways and textured greenery. Palms, olive trees and hedges in various shades of green surrounded the yard's perimeter providing privacy. A smoky glass table, four chairs with jade and coral flowered seat pads and matching sun umbrella were at the end of the pool nearest to the house. At the opposite end of the pool a stout, elderly man was swimming.

"That's Sid in the pool," Myrna said, "Have a seat. I'll get some iced tea," She went back into the house and Julie sat there admiring the unique surroundings.

Sid, who was balding and of impressive stature, rose from the water and hoisted himself onto the rim of the pool. Toweling off at a chaise lounge, he put on a batik shirt and walked over to Julie.

"Hi, I'm Sid, Myrna's husband," he said.

"I'm Julie. I met your wife at the coffee shop. I'm visiting from Pennsylvania."

"You're visiting us?" he said

"No, I was telling Myrna that my mother lived in this neighborhood in 1938 for a year and I always wondered about it," she said.

"1938. I was about thirteen then," he said his eyes looking off in the distance. "A good year, the war hadn't started yet. I lived right here in this house then."

"Really? Did you ever hear of the Nathanson's?"

"The Nathanson's. Sure. Of course, I knew the Nathanson's. On Bedford Drive. Kay still lives there."

Julie felt her limbs weaken at the thought of someone from that family still living here.

Myrna carried out a tray containing a large pitcher and several glass tumblers. "I see you've met Sid," she said.

"Yes, he told me that Kay Nathanson, who my mother cared for, still lives around here.

"Kay Nathanson? Who's that?"

"Kay Beaumont. Used to be a Nathanson," he said.

Myrna frowned at him.

"I can call her to see if she's there," he said to Julie ignoring Myrna.

"We don't need to bother Kay Beaumont," Myrna said.

"Kay wouldn't mind." Sid was already dialing his cell phone. "No one home," Sid said waiting to leave a message. "Kay, it's Sid. Give me a call. I got a gal visiting here says her mother was your babysitter back in 1938." Sid laughed bellicosely on the recorded message. "So give me a call back, Kiddo. Bye."

"That was charming," Myrna said. "He used to date her in high school."

Sid looked very pleased with this memory as he went into the house.

"So you've been getting Christmas cards from Kay Beaumont." Myrna sat down and then paused to light a cigarette; blowing the first puff with such a long breath it seemed to be a comment on Kay. "Kay's alright, I guess, a little Greta Garbo for my taste, if you know what I mean."

Julie didn't know what she meant but was thinking, this is really an adventure. She didn't even know these people. But the prospect of seeing someone who lived with her mother here in Beverly Hills was too much to pass up. She and Myrna talked for over half an hour about the backyard, California palms, wines and shopping.

Sid returned to the patio dressed in a bronze silk shirt and tan slacks looking very dapper. Julie was running out of questions to prolong the conversation and Myrna seemed to be getting bored. This would be the time to say thank you and goodbye but Julie hunkered down. She could sense Sid was on her side as he spun his cell phone around on the table waiting for it to ring and then mercifully, it did.

"Hello," he spoke loudly into the phone, his paunchy face seemed invigorated. "Kay. How are you? Say, I got a gal here says her mother used to be your babysitter." He laughed. "Yeh, yeh. Must have been a long time ago. 1938, she says."

Sid put his hand over the receiver. "Is your mother, Louise?" he asked Julie.

"Yes," she answered.

"Yeh, that's the one," he said.

"O.K. We'll be right over," Sid hung up.

Myrna shifted her weight to one leg, her hand on her hip looking annoyed. "Any chance to see Kay Beaumont," she muttered to Julie. Sid smiled like a man used to getting his way.

Thirty minutes later, Sid, Myrna and Julie were in Kay Beaumont's home on Bedford near Gregory Way. They were led through an impressive foyer to a spacious mostly-white room with beige-tiled floor. The window frames and fireplace were in cherry wood with art nouveau swirls. Four white leather sofas were placed in a square in the middle of an enormous room at an angle to the art deco double doors that led to a veranda and a garden outside. Julie sat on a sofa next to Kay. Large shadows on the walls and floor from the staircase in the foyer, the Corinthian columns that held up the veranda and the fronds from the palm trees in the garden created an eerie film noir atmosphere.

"So you're Louise's girl," Kay said. Her blond and white hair was combed in elegant waves away from her face emphasizing her aristocratic profile which also cast a shadow against the wall. Sid was prancing behind her occasionally giving her a pat on her shoulder. Myrna tried to signal to him but he conveniently looked off in another direction while she arched her eyebrows and frowned.

"I can see some resemblance," Kay said. "Louise was a beauty." She made a grand gesture with her arm like Katherine Hepburn in her early years. "My sister, Sarah, and I thought she was as beautiful as any of the movie stars at the time, like Vivien Leigh. We idolized her. She was only seven years older than me. We told her she should become a movie star. She was flattered, but she was shy and very suspicious of Hollywood I think."

"So she had misgivings about living here," Julie said.

"Oh, no, she loved Beverly Hills. She didn't want to go home but she was summoned by her mother. I believe her mother wired her that her father was dying."

"But my grandfather didn't die until I was in college," Julie said.

"Yes, Louise was really angry when she wrote back about it. It was sheer trickery to get her to return and then there wasn't any easy means for her to come back to Beverly Hills. You didn't have commercial airlines like you do now. Crossing the country by bus was a grueling trip. I believe your father started dating her in earnest when she returned, and after that the war started. With Pearl Harbor, the whole mood of the West coast changed."

Kay rustled over to the white book case across the room in her black silk lounging slacks to retrieve a framed photo, drawing Julie's attention to a diminutive man standing in the corner of the room observing the group. Carrying the picture over to Julie, Kay said, "There's your mother in 1938 next to a Redwood tree and that's me and my sister." Her mother was wearing a shirt-waist dress with shoulder pads and had a serene smile like Ann Blyth. The Nathanson girls were about ten and twelve and stood on either side of her mother looking out toward the camera with impish grins. She was incredulous that there was a photo of her mother displayed in someone's living room here in Beverly Hills.

"Sarah and I always thought Louise would marry Dennis Carter. He was a hot prospect for Warner Brothers," Kay said.

"Dennis Carter?" Julie said and then she had a vague memory of her mother mentioning someone named Dennis. She was beginning to resent Kay's interpretation of her mother's life, her confidence and certainty left no room for ambiguity.

"My mother always said she thought my father looked like Clark Gable when she first met him."

"Yes, she did," Kay said, "We were all star-struck when we first moved out here."

"She returned to marry my father," Julie said.

"Well, eventually, yes," Kay said, "but it was her mother who said she needed her and Louise could not desert her mother. That's my take of it. Her mother summoned her. She said she needed her."

Julie coughed involuntarily. Kay was slinging these

explanations past her like tennis balls. How did this woman know this? And as if Kay was reading her mind, she said, "But you don't have to believe me. It's all in her letters."

"What letters?" Julie said.

"Louise wrote to Sarah and me often and we saved all of them. My husband knows where they are. Wesley, go get the box of letters," she said to the man in the corner who smiled faintly at Julie as he left the room.

"How often did she write?" Julie asked.

"For the first few years about twice a month, then after she got married and had so many kids she was too busy to write and we only got several letters a year."

Wesley came back and said, "The box isn't in the closet. I remember now we moved it to the attic for safe-keeping.

"Well, get Ramon to help you," Kay chided him. Julie sat talking with Kay, Myrna and Sid about her trip to Beverly Hills occasionally choking on her words.

Twenty minutes later Wesley came back with a large carved wooden box which he placed on a coffee table in front of Julie. All gathered around as he unlocked the box and gently pulled it open to reveal about two hundred letters in envelopes. A tear came to Julie's eye as she recognized the unmistakable hand of her mother on the envelopes. She picked up the first and noticed a 1939 post mark stamp. She felt a twinge of jealousy that these strange old people were in possession of so many personal letters from her mother when she had none. Here was a lifetime of letters about a foot deep.

"Would it be possible to photocopy the letters?" she asked Kay.

"Oh, no, dear, they're personal. I don't know if your mother would want you to see them," she said.

Now she was getting angry. Is she saying she can't even read her own mother's letters—letters that would probably answer once and for all why she returned to Pennsylvania and how she felt about it. She had suggested all these damning explanations and now wouldn't even provide the proof.

Kay seemed to sense her outrage and explained, "I've saved these to read in my dotage, when I can't do much else and feel compelled to look back over my life. I can't let them out of my possession and risk losing them."

Sid put his hand on Kay's shoulder again. "She can use our copier. It's just sitting there doing nothing," he said.

"But they're personal letters," Kay said, "Why would you want to read letters to Sarah and me?"

"I'm just perplexed by this question about my mother's life during that year in Beverly Hills. That's why I traveled here," Julie pleaded.

"That's why she traveled here," Sid said hovering behind Kay. Myrna rolled her eyes.

"They're my letters now that my sister is deceased. They were written to us and are meant for our eyes only. I'm sure of it," Kay said.

Julie began to tear up. She wiped her eyes and couldn't help herself. She was distraught.

Kay looked over at her and said, "If you're so intent on reading them, well, that's your decision. But I don't think it's a good idea. There, I've had my say. I guess maybe Wesley could take them over, Sid, and help with the copying. I don't want to lose any," she looked at Sid, furrowing her brow.

"O.K. Wesley can bring them over and stand guard," Sid joked.

"No, I didn't mean that," Kay said waving her hand dismissively.

Wesley stood vigil over the letters, as though someone might try to take one during the distraction of the conversation.

"Wesley, bundle them up and take them over to Sid's to

copy," she said giving him permission. He reclaimed the letter that Julie was holding and gently placed it with the other letters in the bundle.

Sid, Myrna, Julie and Wesley walked back to the Roxbury house, one behind the other like they were in a procession. Sid led with Julie trailing, unable to keep up with his long legs, followed by the more frail-looking Wesley, holding the wooden box in front of him like a sacred icon, and then Myrna, separated from the group to smoke, created the illusion of the incense bearer.

Wesley was all-work while copying the letters and laid down a series of rules.

"You can touch the copies but don't touch the letters."

"Make up piles for each year."

"I'll put the envelopes back into the box."

It was as if Kay had ordained him to be the full-time custodian of her most treasured possession and he accepted this as an honorable role and performed it with resolve.

Three hours after they began, all letters were copied forming a six-inch stack of paper. Sid helped Julie put the stack into an Armani shopping bag.

"Thank you all so much," she said to Sid, Wesley and Myrna. "You've given me something I couldn't have dreamed of."

"Glad to help," Sid said gently tapping her on the back.

"You gonna read all that?" Myrna shook her head sideways, one hand on her hip.

"I will," she said.

Wesley was visibly fatigued from his workload and anxious to bring his day to a close.

* * *

That night in her hotel room Julie began reading.

"Dear Kay, My father is much better. It seems he only had the flu and I suspect my mother just wanted me home. I have

been giving her the cold shoulder for tricking me this way."

"*I miss Beverly Hills already and especially you and Sarah. I guess Dennis and I were not meant to be, too bad. He was so handsome and I think we would have made a good couple. George, my boyfriend here has been pleading with me to marry him but I suspect my life would be very hard if I marry a machinist, although he does look like Clark Gable and that's not half bad. I hope you will be O.K. without me. Anytime you have a problem you can write to me and I will try to help you as much as I can even though I'm 3000 miles away. Love, Louise.*"

So it was all true what Kay said. Her mother returned because of pressure from Julie's grandmother. Her father was her mother's second choice.

Julie continued reading into the late night and early morning. As she read through the years she found things out about her mother that were disconcerting.

"*The doctor said I almost bled to death during the delivery...I never expected this baby ... We're going to name her 'Julie'...*"

And then,

"*I'm returning your money. Not that I'm not grateful. But I want you to know I love you for yourself and not the things your family has given me. I'm sorry I complained about George gambling away his pay check. I borrowed money from my sister and we're getting by O.K.*"

In her forties, she wrote, "*Why, oh, why did my mother call me back here? I'll never forgive her for that. I wish I stayed in Beverly Hills.*"

And even in her sixties after Julie's father died, she wrote, "*I'm glad I have you to write to. I feel I have no close friends but you and your sister and you're 3000 miles away...*"

Her mother had confided in the Nathanson's in Beverly Hills more than in her family or anyone in Pennsylvania. After six hours of this, Julie couldn't take anymore. The whole thing was horrible. She felt the awful mixed emotions of alienation from her mother who didn't even seem to want her, of jealousy of these Beverly Hills' usurpers for her mother's affection, of shame at her mother's near-destitution, of anger at her father for not providing for her mother. The perspective on her life was turned upside down. She had not known her mother at all. She would dread relating all of this to her sisters.

Julie looked at the letters laid out in two piles on the hotel desk, the ones she finished and the ones she had yet to read. If she had a match, she would burn them that instant in the metal wastebasket. She shuddered lest she do something this bold after all the trouble everyone just went through.

She put the "Do Not Disturb" sign on the door and took a sleeping pill and climbed into bed.

Over the next several days she did not touch the two piles of letters. Occasionally she would look at them like they were a web of tarantulas ready to spread throughout the room. Instead of reading the letters, she went back to touring: visiting Santa Barbara one day, spending the following day in funky Venice Beach, then back to the Farmers Market, the tar pits and the Warner Brothers Museum which reminded her of those thirties movies of which her mother was so fond.

One morning she felt mentally well enough to return to The Coffee Bean on Beverly Drive. She had been evading this section of town since she had read the letters.

As she sipped her morning cappuccino, she thought, it was too much information. How much knowledge about our mother, our father do we have a right to—their every thought, their every conversation, their every doubt? We are only one part of their lives. These letters were not meant for her.

A sunbeam fell on her table and she looked upward at the first patch of blue in the sky. She would not read the letters anymore. She would lock them away like Kay did in a box and seek out someone to guard them like Wesley.

"Hi, stranger," Myrna said walking over with Ginger, her cigarette already lit, "haven't seen you around these parts. Were you busy reading those letters?"

"Yes, I think I read one too many," Julie said.

"I knew it was a bad idea," Myrna said. "I get a letter. I read it right over a trash can and drop it in."

"I like your attitude, Myrna. You have the right perspective," Julie said.

"I don't know anything about anything and I want to keep it that way," Myrna said.

"That sounds like a quote from a 1938 movie," Julie laughed.

"It could be," Myrna said. "So what's on the agenda for today?"

"I think I'll go back to the Farmers Market. There's a small Peruvian chest I saw there that I'd like to buy," Julie said.

Stations of the Cross

Brian Feeney moved closer to his den window to view his neighbor's deck below. *I wonder what he's going to do with that,* he thought. Troy Delfino, who rented the house next door, was a soldier, who just returned from Iraq. Leaning upright against the railing on his deck was a large, corroded, bronze cross. Troy was nowhere in sight, so Brian reached for his binoculars on the file cabinet to examine the cross further. The battered crucifix was about four feet high with an 18-inch figure of Christ hanging from it by a thread.

"Looks like he salvaged that from a pile of rubble or something," he said aloud.

"Talking to yourself again?" his wife, Dolores, said entering the room with the morning mail. He flashed a smile at her.

"I was talking to Goldie," he said motioning to their orange cat curled under the desk. This was Brian's running joke with Dolores. He was in the habit of expressing his thoughts out loud as though he had an audience, eliciting droll comments from those in earshot. His chatter was an asset at the Alexandria Hardware Store where he had worked for forty-two years. "All that know-how lost to mankind," he joked when he left.

"Come here. I want you to see something, Dolores." He positioned her in front of him putting his hands on her thin shoulders and then pointed to the cross. Her wavy, platinum hair had the clean scent of shampoo.

"A cross, what's it doing there?" she said. Brian handed her the binoculars. "It's gigantic and so ornate but horrible condition. I bet he got it in Afghanistan," she said.

"He just came back from Iraq, Dolores, not Afghanistan."

"Really, he told me Afghanistan."

"He was in Afghanistan last year but then was redeployed to Iraq again," Brian said. "I was just talking to that Bozo consultant on the other side of him last week and he told me Troy just returned from Iraq and he got the Purple Heart. Imagine. We're living next to an American hero."

"Don't you have to get wounded for The Purple Heart? ... I hope he's OK." She gave the binoculars to Brian. "I mean who could keep track of all the places he's been stationed. He told Pete he was stationed in Germany too."

Pete was their thirty-five year old son who spent most of his time at a computer working on some hush-hush program for the government. Now that he was retired, Brian wanted to spend more time with Pete to coax him into doing something outdoors in the sun for gosh sake—he was thinking, fishing in the Blue Ridge maybe. Pete spent too much time alone—didn't seem to have a lot of friends, not like his old man at his age. He was becoming one of those fast-food, obese, computer geeks who use less than five words when they talk. Not that Brian was in such good shape himself. But at least at the hardware store he did physical work hauling around peat moss and lumber, and bathtubs, and you name it. He finally had to quit because his back kept going out on him.

Brian resumed staring at the cross with his binoculars. "I don't like this, Dolores. Something strange is going on. He used to be pretty friendly when I would bump into him. Not now. One deployment too many, I think."

"He seems very polite," she said, "especially compared to a lot of kids nowadays. Although I saw a TV show about how a lot of these soldiers are coming home with PTSD. Do you think Troy could have PTSD?"

"PTSD, Come on," Brian waved his hand dismissively, but the thought occurred to him too. Where was Troy's old girlfriend? He hadn't seen her around lately.

"Well, stop staring with those; he'll see you," Dolores cautioned him, "Or at least move away from the window."

"He's not even there," Brian said. "You can go now." He motioned her away as he continued spying on his mysterious neighbor.

The next day Dolores was taking the trash out when she encountered Troy cleaning the intricate cross with a barbecue brush. "Hi, Troy, nice cross. Where'd you get it?"

"Good Morning, Ma'am. I got it overseas," Troy mumbled and turned away while he continued to remove the grime stuck in the crevices of the cross. He was clad only in a pair of long black shorts. On his bronzed muscular back he had a symmetric tribal tattoo, broad swirls radiating outward from a curved cross in the center. He was tall and lean, all muscle. His dark hair always looked wet and sleek like he had just been swimming. He had a handsome Italian face with a Roman nose and dark, deep-set eyes.

"Very impressive," she said as she returned to her deck. She noticed an 8-inch gash of scar tissue visible on his right calf.

"Thank you, Ma'am," he said not looking at her.

* * *

"I'm telling you," Brian said to Dolores at supper, "the way they treat these guys now, deploying them here one year, giving them a few months off, and then sending them to another place, is asking for trouble."

"I said it was very impressive. But he didn't want to talk. It was odd," Dolores said.

"There's nothing to worry about, Dolores," Brian kissed her on the cheek. "Oh, here's Pete. Pete, Pete, my boy. Do we have a story for you!"

"Another one," Pete laughed. He was a massive presence in the small kitchen, dwarfing his mother and at eye level with the top of the refrigerator. He hugged her warmly, patting her on the head to emphasize their height difference.

"Let me get you a plate," Dolores said.

"I can't stay long," Pete said sitting down.

"So, fishing, Dad. Lake Moomaw. Do they have cell phone coverage there at Moomaw?" Pete teased his father.

"Oh, yeah, big satellite dishes all over the mountains, relaying everything, everywhere." Brian said motioning broadly with his arms. "Everything's ready, Pete. Catch and release; that's what they call it. If we don't go to Moomaw, then Hidden Valley is great." Brian wanted to make certain they went this time. "Beautiful country, but no commo there; it's like in the old days."

"No, I want to tell everyone in the office I spent the weekend at Lake Moomaw," Pete laughed.

Dolores gave Pete a generous portion of pot roast. "Thanks, Mom. Looks good."

"Oh, but if we go in the summer, the trout don't bite at Moomaw," Brian said frowning. Dolores and Pete smiled at each other as Brian became more expressive.

"I know. We can go to Cowpasture River and fish for bass or perch; what do you think, Pete?"

Pete laughed. "Cowpasture River would be a close second to Moomaw."

Watch. He'll cancel at the last minute again, Brian thought. Yes, he was a top-notch engineer and had to work long hours and Brian was proud of him, but couldn't he spend a little time with his old man.

"Hey, you know, Pete, what Troy has on his deck?"

"Let him eat, Brian," Dolores said.

"What, does Troy have on his deck?"

"He's got this four-foot cross from overseas. You should see it; it's pure bronze, I think, and rich-looking with curly-cues all over it. But it looks like it's been in the war, I bet."

"He's obsessed with this cross," Dolores said to Pete, "But I do think there's something odd about the whole thing."

"You worry about nothing. It's exciting. I bet it was on a church steeple or maybe on the altar. Imagine. You can see it upstairs from the den window, Pete."

"I gotta see this." Pete rose from the table and ran upstairs.

"Now his dinner will get cold," Dolores chided Brian.

"Don't worry about it. He doesn't care if it's hot. He'll eat anything; he'll eat this brochure here." He waved a brochure on "Fishing in a National Forest."

Pete thundered down the steps after a few minutes and said, "Awesome cross. It looks like it came from a church. Do you think maybe it could have been from a church bombed in Iraq? That would be major."

"Who knows? Could be. He's been stationed there twice," Brian said raising two fingers.

Everyday thereafter, Brian monitored the cross on the deck; he told Dolores he was going to the den to write a check for the dentist or the car insurance or to use the computer. He would position himself behind the hutch on top of his desk with his binoculars, similar to a bird watcher in a blind, giving him cover for his clandestine operation. At first there was nothing happening with the cross; it was stationary, leaning against the railing next to the broom on the deck. Then he noticed small objects on the deck by the cross, brushes, rags, pails, a screwdriver, a hammer and on occasion Troy himself would be out on his deck puttering with the cross.

One day Brian was in the den for over an hour watching Troy work on the cross. At the hardware shop he joked that men love to watch each other work, so he had no qualms about spying on Troy. Troy was laboring with such devotion, being careful he didn't cause permanent damage to an object already crumbling away. He applied a small amount of a cleaning agent to an inch at a time and then he'd examine his work closely.

"He should be using Kruegers' degreaser. These young guys nowadays don't have the know-how," Brian said. I should go down there and tell him, he thought, but then decided it might be awkward especially after Troy's uneasy encounter with Dolores.

When Troy was through for the day, he gently positioned the cross against the deck railing so it was secure; he stooped down with one knee on the deck for several minutes, his back to Brian, first fixing the cross in place and then bowed his head almost as though he was in prayer.

Brian became anxious about the situation the next week when he spotted a large blade hunting knife on the ledge of the deck. "That's probably a fifteen inch blade," Brian said. Troy was shirtless as usual, brandishing his Amazon-tribe tattoo, looking threatening, yet spectacular, like a gladiator. Then he put on goggles and took out a blow torch; Brian could see he was loosening the soldering metal that fastened the figure of Christ to the cross. "I guess he's taking it off," Brian said. Soon the contorted figure of Christ was detached and Troy put it on the deck ledge next to the knife. "He shouldn't leave that there," Brian said shaking his head.

A few days passed and Brian heard a loud gasp from Dolores upstairs. She came hurrying down. "Mother of God! He took Jesus off the cross. Jesus is lying there like—like a Barbie doll. It looks awful." As Brian had suspected, Dolores had also become an active observer of the cross and Troy's activity; on occasion he had found his binoculars out of place.

"He's refurbishing the whole thing. Can't you see? Calm down, Dolores."

Over the next two months -- well into July—the Feeney's kept watch over Troy's painstaking cleaning and restoration of the bronze cross. They admired his progress and Brian softened his criticism. Where there were missing or bent parts of metal, Troy somehow found a way to restore them. Dolores' fears were allayed and instead she commented on his beautiful back with its striking cross tattoo and how his leg was a scar of honor. Brian admired Troy's patience with the most minor details of the cross. Watching was mesmerizing; Troy did everything in silence—no music playing, no friends watching him, except clandestinely by Brian, Dolores and Pete who would always ask, "How's the cross coming?" each time he visited. After Troy soldered the glistening figure of Christ back on the cross, the three of them were in the den passing around the binoculars.

But one day Goldie wandered over to Troy's deck and took an interest in the cross—as though she was part of the Feeney observation crew except, being Goldie, she took a flying leap and landed square on the figure of Christ, knocking the whole cross down onto Troy's deck with a deafening crash. Troy sprang from his door, grabbed his long-blade hunting knife, and tore after Goldie who ran swiftly off the deck with Troy in pursuit. Having heard the noise, Dolores ran outside and saw Troy running after Goldie with the knife thrust out in front of him.

"Stop it. Stop it, Troy. What's wrong with you? Are you crazy?" she yelled.

"Keep your cat away from my cross," he scowled and retreated to his deck, taking the steps two at a time as he went to recover his fallen cross. He examined each section reverently while he cleaned it with soapy water. Afterwards, he took the cross inside his house.

"You have to go over there," Dolores said to Brian when he came home." He was acting crazy. Thank God I was there or he would have killed Goldie, I'm sure. What if he has PTSD; soldiers with PTSD have shot whole families. It's all those back-to-back stations. You don't think he has a gun, do you?"

"Why was Goldie outside in the first place?" Brian said. He was deflecting her question because he had seen a gun cabinet in Troy's house when he was visiting him the previous year.

"She got out—OK, I don't know how."

* * *

Brian waited on the small cement front porch of the Cape Cod house for Troy to answer the doorbell which Brian had rung twice. Through force of habit he shook the black wrought-iron railing to see how sturdy it was. He rang again. After the fourth ring Troy opened the door and Brian greeted him with a broad smile. Once inside he got to the issue quickly.

"You know how women are, Troy. They're emotional. They get upset over knives and things guys know you need for survival tactics. Am I right?" Troy glared at him. Brian ambled around a bit, using his hand gestures, giving Troy a chance to explain.

"The cat jumped on my cross—jumped right on it."

"Right, you're right, Troy. But Goldie's a cat; you can't control animals; you know that. She's supposed to stay in the house. But she snuck out. After all, the cross was outside and who knows what other small animals are running around here at night. There was a raccoon family down in the ravine area and possums are around," Brian said.

"This is a holy cross," Troy said softly. Then he said very slowly, "Four of my buddies died right near this cross in Iraq."

"My God, Troy! What happened?"

Troy paced in his living room looking away. "They went to a Christian church in Iraq to help the police." He motioned with his arm, a pained look on his face and said, voice-breaking, "The whole church was leveled." He continued to pace. Brian had his hand covering his mouth. And then in a steady voice Troy said, "Nothing was left of my four buddies. It was like they weren't even there. Some dog tags, a few bones—not enough to even bury in Arlington," he mumbled weakly.

"That's terrible, Troy! Awful."

"All I could find there was this cross which I took and hid. Some guys in Transportation Corps who knew my buddies helped to ship it to the States."

Both men paused and said nothing for several minutes.

Then Brian said, "What're you going to do with the cross, Troy?"

"I don't know. I was going to put it here in the yard but if your cat and everyone else's cats or dogs are going to molest it, I guess I can't do that now." His eyes hardened and he was clenching his teeth.

Brian tried to shift his attention from the cat. "Could you get it into Arlington Cemetery, do you think or on one of the Army bases?"

"No, they'd never let me. I'm not even supposed to have it," he said.

"Yeah, I guess you can't put it in any official place—like a church cemetery or anything," Brian said waving his hand and pacing.

Troy slumped into a chair wearily. Brian said, "Did you guys have anyplace special you always went?"

He waited awhile for Troy to mumble, "We'd go to bars on the base to blow off steam. Not the place to put a cross."

"No. You don't want to put a cross in a bar," Brian said.

"You never went on any outings together? Any road trips maybe?

He waited awhile for Troy to reply. "Right before we went to Iraq, we went hunting in the George Washington Forest. We got a bear there during hunting season. The guys were pretty proud; it was the first time for each of us."

"A bear, wow! You got a bear? That's something. Hey, why not put the cross there in the forest where you found the bear." Brian was brainstorming now.

The gleaming cross was in the living room leaning against the gun cabinet. Troy motioned toward it. "How would I manage? The cross is almost a hundred pounds."

"You'd need to put it in concrete; otherwise, it would tumble over," Brian said.

"I smuggled it out so I can't ask any guys I know for help. I don't want anyone else to get in trouble," Troy said.

"I can help you, Troy." Brian volunteered. "I don't mind getting in trouble," he winked. He saw a glimpse of lightness going through Troy's face. Brian knew he couldn't handle this job alone and in an instant he had to decide on whether to get his son involved. His instinct said yes. "I'll get my boy, Pete, to help us too. He'd help. I'm sure." Brian waved his hand like it was settled. He hoped he could convince Pete how important this was. "It'll be a memorial for your buddies, Troy."

"A memorial, yes," Troy stammered.

* * *

They started loading the truck early the following Saturday to drive to the mountains. Brian had persuaded Dolores to visit her sister in New Jersey. "Pete and I will be fishing anyway," he said. It was a little white lie he reasoned. He cautioned Pete not to tell his mother. "She's a worry wart."

Brian had loaded all the tools and supplies they would need

to erect the cross in the forest and closed the back of the truck. Troy ran into his house to get something and Brian was dismayed when he came out with a hunting rifle. Troy squirreled it into a space in the back. "In case we see bears or something," he said to Brian who had a gaping expression.

They were quiet during the drive to the mountains, talking now and then about baseball, football, not much about their mission. Brian had mixed feeling that Pete had shown up for once; usually he got a last minute phone call with some excuse from Pete. Now here he was conversing with Troy on PC's, giving him some tips on routers and software. But why did Troy have to bring that damn rifle, Brian thought.

Brian tried to shake off his misgivings. "So we're on Old Forge Road now," he said, driving his truck through the George Washington National Forest. "Once we get to the pull-off area we'll have to haul the cross and the rest of the materials a couple miles uphill."

"Yes, Sir," Troy said, "but I'll carry the cross. You'll have the wheelbarrow for the rest."

Brian knew this wouldn't be easy on a hiking trail and there was his unreliable back. He said, "I don't think you can carry that cross the whole way by yourself, Troy. Pete, maybe you can help steady it some."

"Sure. I don't mind sharing the load even. We can change off every fifteen minutes," Pete volunteered.

They found the pull-off area at one o'clock in the afternoon. Brian tried to conceal the truck by hiding it in a thicket of bushes. They gathered their equipment and took a heavy duty lamp; it would be dark before they completed their mission and got back to the truck.

After the long ride Brian's back was hurting so he put on his hardware store heavy-lifting brace. He looked over to see Troy loading an eight-round clip into his rifle.

"Why don't you let me put the rifle in the wheel barrow, Troy?" Brian said. Troy looked over at him and at the heavy cross and nodded OK.

Troy and Pete tried several ways to hold both ends of the cross but it became apparent that Troy had to put it over his shoulder; Pete held the longer part trailing behind him when the path got rocky. Troy took most of the weight, so Pete also carried a pick ax and a heavy bag of tools. Brian put the concrete in the wheelbarrow with several gallons of water, a shovel and other items they would need.

They trudged up the hill, on an overgrown path. Sometimes Brian had trouble getting the wheel barrel over the rocks or tree roots on the trail but Pete was there to lend a hand, his large presence clearly an asset. They stopped to search for the trees Troy and his buddies spray-painted with red X's on the path where they got the bear. The hike was going slowly. With their heavy load, the hot weather, and looking for the X's, they were stopping to rest every ten minutes. They were quiet as they walked and could sense the forest: chipmunks darting through the dried leaves, birds calling, small branches falling to the forest floor. Brian was starting to feel woozy from the heat and was wondering if he would make it.

Once Troy stumbled and fell with the cross but Pete helped him up and then retrieved the fallen cross and placed it gently on Troy's shoulder; strands of Troy's sweat-drenched hair hung loosely down the side of his face. He pushed them aside with the back of his hand smudging his face with dirt. Brian lent him a bandana to wipe his face.

They marched uphill from tree to tree until they found the critical trunk painted with an encircled X, red rays leading out from a circle resembling the sun in a child's drawing.

"Here it is," Troy said, "Behind this tree. I remember it was near the mountain peak."

They looked around for a while, trying to find a spot that was soft enough to dig a hole. Pete began loosening the dirt with the pick ax he had been carrying; Troy began digging with the trenching shovel. Brian got the rest of the materials ready: gravel for the base of the hole, garden edging for around the top, a ground sleeve for the middle of the hole to encase the cross, the quick drying concrete and the water he lugged in his wheelbarrow.

After Pete and Troy completed the digging, Brian went to work with building the concrete base. He worked swiftly asking each of the other men for assistance when he needed it. And then suddenly he collapsed. "Christ," he mumbled looking up at Troy and Pete; they were both looking down at him concerned, trying to get him to drink some water. He threw up once but the two guys continued to give him water and after thirty minutes he was able to regain his senses and sit against a tree trunk.

"We can do the rest, Dad," Pete said.

"Tell us how and we'll do everything," Troy added, "You sit there and sip some water. You're dehydrated; I saw a lot of guys like that in Iraq. You'll be O.K."

Brian felt shaky and disoriented. He espied the rifle on the ground several feet away. He turned to Troy and Pete and told them to insert the cross into the ground sleeve. Troy sealed the base with more concrete and slanted it slightly away from the sleeve with the trowel while Pete held the cross steady in an upright position. Brian insisted they stand one on one side and one on the other holding the cross erect until the concrete hardened. Troy and Pete talked casually while they held the cross upright for about twenty minutes. Afterwards they packed dirt around the base to further stabilize the mounted cross. To Brian they looked like two young men anyone would be proud of—strong, capable, and respectful. When he felt that he was recovering, he struggled to stand up and went over to the cross grinning at them, still feeling a little woozy.

Brian felt the top of the cross and said, "That'll hold. No one will be able to budge this." They were sweating profusely, so toweled off with old rags Brian had brought along.

Then Troy slumped down to the ground next to the cross and said, "I should have been with them that day. I was sick in quarters recovering from this shrapnel in my leg so I couldn't go." The men were quiet for several minutes and then Brian said, "Think of this, Troy. Maybe you were spared to memorialize these men."

Brian went over and picked up Troy's rifle. He felt a need to show his trust in Troy. "Why not give your friends a 3-volley salute, Troy." He handed the rifle to Troy who got up, took the gun and walked several yards away from the cross. He lifted the rifle in the air and fired it three times creating three loud blasts that reverberated in the hills.

The three men then composed themselves and stood in front of the cross for several minutes in silent prayer.

A few rays of the setting sun fell on the cross which glistened in the quiet green forest, the smell of fresh earth permeating the air. "They would like this, I think," Troy said.

"You're a loyal soldier, Troy, salvaging the cross, restoring it like you did. It's beautiful right here in the forest." Brian said, putting his hand on Troy's shoulder. He turned and looked over at his own son who was still packing the dirt around the cross with his feet. Brian smiled; he felt so happy at this accomplishment and that his son was here with him. He looked up at the cross which gleamed brightly from the setting sun. How brilliant it looked here among the old forest trees that soared upward into the heavenly sky.

Meditating like Brutus

My mother who was thirty-nine and too old to have children was going to have one anyway. I can't tell you how much this annoyed me and worse than that made me positively ill with worry because her doctor told her she would probably die and her baby would probably die too.

I was a sophomore in the 1960 fall semester at Bishop O'Connor High School in Evanston, Pennsylvania and lived in the next town over in Barboursville. I had to take the city bus to school since it was five miles from home plus I had to walk the last mile from the Dunbar Street bus stop being that my mother made me get off at a stop light instead of where my friends got off which meant I had to walk home alone.

On a cold November afternoon, I got off the bus carrying a book bag with five heavy text books dreading the long walk home which was quite boring because the houses I walked past were all similar, old two-story coal-mining houses upgraded with ridiculous siding and front porches as wide as the house to hold their all-weather gliding sofas.

The day before, my mother told Doreen and me, "I may not be here much longer, girls, so you better do what I say while I'm still here or you'll regret it when I'm dead." I felt shaken when she said this even though I knew she really meant it for Doreen, my thirteen year-old sister, because I was about the most obedient person in Barboursville and Doreen was the opposite.

I could hardly stand it because Doreen was always getting yelled at by my parents and I couldn't concentrate on math and Shakespeare with all that commotion in the house. We were studying Julius Caesar in school and Sister Damian had a long discussion on how stoical the ancient Romans were. Brutus was so stoical he never even cried when his beloved wife Portia died a horrible death from swallowing hot coal. Barboursville had its own coal mine so I could imagine what a terrible death that had to be. How I wished I could be as stoical as Brutus if my mother died. Brutus said "with meditating that Portia die once" he was able to endure her death when it finally happened.

As I turned the corner onto Oak Street passing by Romano's grocery store, I saw Sonny Peterson who I think was buying cigarettes and he waved to me through the large plate glass window. I waved back even though I hardly ever talked to him because he was three years older than me.

Romano's was my signal to begin my ritual thinking like Brutus. I meditated trying to imagine a black hearse in front of our house and black crepe draping the door. In Barboursville they often buried you right from your house instead of from a funeral home. Sometimes I would walk down a street and see a house decorated in black bunting around the doorway or in the front window. It was a particularly muddy black, like it had been stored in an attic waiting for the next death and was fading.

I came around the bend from Oak Street onto Sycamore Street where we lived and looked across the way several houses down and was relieved to see no hearse, no sign of black trim anywhere. I breathe a sigh of relief and remained stoical like Brutus. The light was on in the living room which meant Doreen was probably home but my father's car wasn't there yet. Doreen was tall for thirteen, and with her long blond hair could easily have passed for fifteen, my age, so maybe that's why my father became so obsessed with her whereabouts, calling her "boy-crazy," and trailing a block behind her in his car like he was a private eye when she mentioned she was going for a walk which made him a very poor spy because we had the only pink car in Barboursville.

I crept up to our house cautiously because I never knew for sure my mother was alright until I saw her very pregnant body. At this point I had been practicing my Brutus meditation for two months; I only hoped I was meditating correctly since Shakespeare didn't have detailed instructions on this, not even in the footnotes. Mrs. Sampson who lived next door and was outside raking leaves said, "Hi, Vicky." I waved back.

"Vicky! Vicky! Mom had a baby boy!" Doreen burst out the front door just as I walked up the steps. She was smiling broadly just the opposite of her usual teenage misery look.

"Oh, is it a boy? I bet your father's glad," Mrs. Sampson shouted to us from her yard.

"What about Mom?" I asked.

"She's OK, I think" Doreen said.

"Are they OK?" Mrs. Sampson asked as she walked over to us.

"I think so," Doreen said.

This really floored me! Why leave an important message like this with a scatterbrain like Doreen; now I would have to wait for my father to come home or until he called again.

"So now we have a little brother, I guess," I said to Doreen, who was putting her coat on, as I was taking mine off.

"That's what Dad told me—a brother. Get the phone if he calls back. I'm going for a walk," she said.

Well, I tried to make conversation with her as my mother asked but she would rather visit one of her boyfriends while my father wasn't around. I hoped it was Will Carney around the corner on Oak Street and not Sonny Peterson since my father really hated when she went to see Sonny because he was five years older than Doreen. I was sent to check up on her and Sonny one time and all I saw was Doreen sitting on his front porch steps and Sonny laughing while he polished his car. But Sonny joked with everyone, probably because he was around a lot being that he was on disability for some kidney problem. One time Sonny teased me when I got my hair cut too short. "What happened to you? Did you get scalped?" he said. I hated the haircut and knew it was too short so I almost started to cry which Sonny noticed and then said, "Looks nice, Vicky."

It took a while before I realized there was to be no black: no black hearse, no black crepe, no standing at the grave site by my mother's coffin and maybe a little tiny coffin for the baby, all things I had meditated on for months and was ready for. But, of course, it was a relief, and I was grateful that Shakespeare had taught me to meditate and to be calm at such times and to be stoical like the ancient Romans.

When my father brought my mother and the new baby home the next day, everyone gathered around him like he was a little prince.

"Look how smooth his skin is," I said, "Such teeny fingers and toes."

"Doesn't he smell sweet?" my mother said; she seemed healthy and cheerful. The baby had lovely blue eyes with blond fuzz on his head, the cutest little boy. He was to be named Robert after my father but everyone was already calling him Bobby.

"Could I pick Bobby up," Doreen said as my mother handed him off. "He's not too heavy. I can carry him easy."

Next my father took the baby and started to sing to him, "Climb up on my knee, Sonny Boy, 'Though you're only three, Sonny Boy...'" This was typical of my father who sang Al Jolson songs around the house in full voice any time he was in the mood.

I said, "Dad, you're going to scare Bobby. He's not used to your loud singing like we are." My mother just laughed.

My Dad said, "He loves it. Look at him." Bobby was cooing and seemed to be enjoying my father's singing.

My interest in little Bobby began to wane as he became more trouble than entertainment. He either had to be changed or was spitting up or screaming like a banshee while I was trying to solve a math problem.

Doreen didn't seem to mind as much because for one thing she never studied and then again she might have been thinking in a few more years she would be having her own little boy with maybe Sonny Peterson and this was good practice for that.

"Everybody has to help around here now," my mother said.

"I can clean the bathroom," I quickly offered because I really didn't want to take care of Bobby and the bathroom was enormous being that my father knocked down a closet wall making the bathroom as wide as the house so I thought this would be enough but my mother looked at me like it wasn't, so I added, "and the dining room." She still didn't respond so I said, "And I'll do all the ironing including Dad's white shirts and our dresses."

"OK," my mother accepted this final deal which I knew she would because my mother just hated ironing and I didn't mind it, being that I could memorize poems while I ironed or science notes or I could just turn on the radio and listen to the Top 40 and memorize the songs I liked which I would mimic for my friends at Bishop O'Connor dances. "Tears on my Pillow" by Little Anthony was one of my favorites.

Then Doreen said, "I can take care of Bobby when I'm not in school," This is the answer my mother wanted, so she was positively overjoyed with Doreen, giving her a hug which Doreen just shrugged off.

Maybe because there were several older people in the house,

Bobby grew up at a fast pace. He was quite an independent kid, but a troublemaker too. "Where's Bobby?" was the constant question from my mother when Bobby was about two and I was a Freshman day-hop at nearby Mercy College where I majored in math but also took many courses in the liberal arts because I loved literature and art but I figured math would be better for getting a good job someplace where there wasn't a coal mine.

Doreen said, "I can't be with him every single minute of the day."

"It's not your fault, Doreen," my mother said, "Bobby is just full of energy."

"If we get rid of the table in the dining room, I can block off half the room and give him his own play area," my father proposed.

"But where will we eat?" I asked.

"We can eat at the kitchen table until Bobby gets older," my father said, "I'll just put the dining table in the basement." It seemed excessive to me but I generally tried to steer clear of any Bobby issues.

So my father began a two-week project of building a play-pen for Bobby that would divide the dining room in half and include the piano on Bobby's side. How did they expect me to study English literature or math with Bobby banging on the piano all the time?

My father finally finished the wall to keep Bobby imprisoned. It was constructed out of two layers of plywood with a wide ledge on top which my father didn't even bother to paint. It was a monstrosity! I don't know why I expected anything better from my father. All of his solutions to problems were like this, practical with no consideration for beauty. I decided right then never to invite any of my college friends over to our house.

"Okay, Bobby, come over here. You get half the dining room to play in plus the piano," my father said pleased with his "wall." Bobby looked happy probably thinking this was a new game as my father lifted him up and put him into his new playpen.

Bobby ran back and forth like the wild child he was and right before our eyes tore to the piano stool, shoved it to the barricade, climbed on the stool and from there onto the "wall" and was back among us.

"You little monkey," my father said. My mother just went into the kitchen. She was used to my father's dreadful inventions.

So Bobby still kept running around the house and getting into trouble. Once he was rushing to go downstairs and he tripped and hit his forehead on the banister in the hallway. There was so much blood we had to take him to the emergency room of the Evanston Hospital for five stiches on his forehead which would "scar him for life," my mother said.

"You'll look like a pirate," I said and he seemed pleased.

"This little boy is going to be the death of me," my mother said. There she was with the dying again. At such times I meditated like Brutus, even though it looked like Bobby was more at risk of dying than my mother.

As Bobby got older he became quite resourceful for a little kid and went about his business like any of us. Everyone tried, but no one could get up as early as Bobby. I was getting ready one morning to go to college and came downstairs for breakfast and found Bobby, at the age of three, making a pitcher of Kool-Aid for the family.

"What are you doing, Bobby?" I asked as I caught him standing on the stool by the kitchen sink filling a pitcher with water, the empty Kool-Aid envelope on the counter.

"Making Kool-Aid. It's for everybody," he answered. I had fearful visions of sticky Kool-Aid covering the floor but he managed to move stools around, open the refrigerator and put the pitcher inside. I had seen it in the refrigerator before and wondered how it had gotten there.

Doreen was now in high school and had to catch the bus on Dunbar Street so she was out of the house early. I was left with Bobby, who settled in to watch Captain Kangaroo as I was waiting for my carpool to Mercy College. It was tempting to tease Bobby by treating him as a little adult since he seemed to want to be one.

"What do you think Wordsworth meant when he said, "The world is too much with us," I asked him.

"I don't know. I'm just a little boy." He had his eyes transfixed on Captain Kangaroo.

"I don't believe Captain Kangaroo is a kangaroo at all," I'd tease him.

"Stop it. I want to watch this." He tried to swat me away.

When my ride came I quoted Robert Frost, "I'm going out to clean the pasture spring. I'll only stop to rake the leaves away."

"Go. Go."

Still he persisted with his heart-stopping behavior. One Saturday I was in the living room with my mother, Doreen and Bobby. "Today we're going to do some spring cleaning so we need to air out the room," my mother said opening the front door and the windows. It was unseasonably warm outside.

Bobby was bouncing up and down on the winged-back chair and my mother said, "Stop that, Bobby." Bobby stopped for a second and then resumed jumping on the chair. As my mother took the cushions out of the sofa with Doreen watching her, I looked over and saw the winged-back chair tip backward against the opened window and Bobby tumble out the window which was twelve feet above the ground. I was sure my little brother had just died; his previously charmed life had finally come to a close. I was speechless, horrified and I didn't know how to tell my mother and sister about Bobby's demise and then the little devil came bounding in the front door with a big smile on his face.

"I fell out," he said laughing. My mother and sister looked up bewildered.

"You're a bad boy, Bobby, jumping on the chair like that. See what can happen," I yelled at him as I examined him for any injuries. "Why can't you listen to Mom?" My heart was still pounding as I was the lone witness to his hurdling out the window. I tried to meditate like Brutus to be stoical and to calm my beating heart.

Luckily school was about to end so Doreen could spend more time babysitting Bobby.

"I know what you're up to with your evening walks with Bobby," I said to her.

"Do you want to take him?" she asked.

"No. But I know you're visiting your boyfriends and using him as an excuse," I said.

"You can take care of him anytime you like," she said.

I decided to let it be, lest I get stuck with Bobby who was a full time job to watch; he never sat still for too long, and I was not into physical activity. Besides, I was planning to take an elective course in World Literature the next semester at Mercy College and I wanted to start on the required reading, particularly the Greek tragedies. Being a science major I had to get a jump on my electives during the summer.

But then Bobby came down with a strange malady. He would cry out, "My legs! My legs!" He was four going on five but small for his age because he only ate Chef Boyardee Spaghetti-O's; nothing else appealed to him. Occasionally Doreen would carry him back from their long walks to her boyfriends' houses because his legs hurt so much.

I stooped down and massaged his legs and said, "Does it help if I rub them, Bobby?"

"No, they hurt. They hurt," he cried dancing around. I felt sorry for him as he sought our help but there was nothing we could do.

My mother took him to the Doctor who said he wasn't getting enough Vitamin D, probably because he preferred Kool-Aid to milk. He got shots or vitamins to help with his legs, but I worried about him all summer in between reading the Greek tragedies.

Still he seemed to like going with Doreen on her after-supper strolls. And my father thought of Bobby as a chaperone for Doreen as she toured the town stopping at this boyfriend's house one day, and another boyfriend's the next day. Usually she stayed outside in plain sight while her love interests were working on their car which was a favorite pastime for Barboursville guys.

I was enjoying the summer, meeting up with my college friends at the Red Roof Diner where we discussed our escape plans from Barboursville, or watching interleague baseball games at the Barboursville baseball diamond with my neighborhood friends to root for the Sampson boy next door, or just laying outside on the chaise lounge reading under the cherry tree. My mother would bring me lemonade or cookies while I sat outside reading for hours. The summer had been almost languorous.

One evening I was sitting on the steps of our front porch watching the world go by slowly. In Barboursville there was very little foot or car traffic but just enough to keep you on the lookout for people you knew. I heard an odd noise from down the street like a whelp from a sick dog, a strange sound. As I sat there it grew louder. I looked next door at Mrs. Sampson who was watering her roses in the shade of the early evening.

"Did you hear something, Vicky?" she asked.

"Yes, coming from that direction," I answered and got up to look far down Sycamore Street as she did too.

"Isn't that Doreen?" she said. I made out a small figure not an inch visible from there."

"It looks like she's carrying Bobby," Mrs. Sampson said. The sound became louder and louder as Doreen and Bobby got closer. People up and down the street were now emerging from their homes as it became apparent she was crying, screaming, howling. Never had I heard such a sound. As she got closer, Bobby could be heard whimpering like a sick animal. Mrs. Sampson said, "Get your mother. Quick"

I rushed inside and called my mother, "There's something wrong with Bobby. Doreen is screaming outside. She's carrying him." My mother tore out of the house and with Mrs. Sampson we converged on Doreen and Bobby who were nearing our block now with the horrible aura of tragedy about them. When we got to them, Doreen put Bobby down and we glanced at him perplexed as he tore right by us and scampered back home, up the steps and into the house. My mother tried to find out what was wrong with Doreen but it seemed impossible as she clung to my mother almost pulling her down.

"What is it? What is it?" The whole neighborhood wanted to know. Doreen cried and screamed so desperately her face contorted in a pattern of horror. My mother and Mrs. Sampson led her back to our house and it wasn't until we were inside that Doreen choked on her words and said, "He died. He's dead. Sonny's dead." She continued to moan emitting an awful sound and kept beating her breasts as in a Greek tragedy, her long blond hair falling forward over her contorted face. Little by little she told us she had gone to visit Sonny as she did two days before, but as she got to his house she saw a black hearse, with its black-draped windows, in front of Sonny's house, with Sonny's dead body being carried out right in front of her, his mother in the open doorway sobbing loudly.

"Oh, my God!" I said sitting down on the couch; I was

shaken. This was the horrible scene I had once imagined for my mother and brother five years earlier when my brother was born and when I first began to meditate on my mother's death like Brutus did for Portia's. My little brother was like the portent of death after all, only it was my sister who chanced upon her longtime friend's body being taken away at the precise moment she arrived at his door to meet with him. It was staggering; instead of her friendly chat with her boyfriend she saw his sad dead body emerging from his home in a basket, Sonny's lifeless body visible to her.

What is the probability that one could chance upon a loved one's departure from this earth? Miniscule, I learned in my Math classes. But my sister would have to go through her life thinking otherwise. There would be no erasing this image from her memory through meditation or logical persuasion or future happiness. I moved next to her on the couch and placed my arm around her shoulder and took her hand in mine as she sobbed steadily, but she would not be comforted. After a period she retreated to her bedroom and closed the door where we could hear her weeping throughout the long night. No one could persuade her that there was not more cruelty to come.

Of Persimmons and Asian Pears

I am walking through the parking lot at Eden Center when I
hear a voice that sends chills up my spine.

"Linh Hoa. Linh Hoa."

I turn slowly and look into the smiling face of my ex, Tai
Chinh.

"I knew that was you, Linh Hoa," Tai stammers, "I said to
myself who else is so petite and holds her back so straight like
a ballroom dancer."

"Hello, Tai."

I can't go anywhere in the Northern Virginia Vietnamese
community without running into my ex, our families or our
friends. I feel suffocated.

A lively crowd of six young Vietnamese heading to a popu-
lar restaurant in Eden Center passes close to us. I smile at them.
They remind me of my youth in Hue, the ancient capital and
most beautiful city in Vietnam. I am 35 now but I don't feel any
older than when I left Vietnam in 1975 during the fall of Saigon.
I was fifteen then.

"Did you eat yet? We can go to Eden Cafe for lemongrass
chicken." Tai suggests. He is wearing a worn, faded suit with
a soiled tie. His glasses and haircut are outdated but I know he
does not care about such things.

"Oh, I ate already. I stopped to get this video," I say showing

121

him a Vietnamese movie. It is seven in the evening and I am starving.

"I sold our townhouse, but I had to get out by end August. So I sleep now on my office floor." He laughs nervously. "My apartment is not ready until first December."

"Tai, you can't sleep on your office floor for three months."

"It is not too bad. I have Yoga mat. And you know I sleep three, four hours a night anyway."

"Why don't you move in with your mother until December?"

"Going to work would take ninety minutes. This way there is no commute." He laughs again. "And if I cannot sleep at night, I work on case file."

I can picture him waking at four in the morning and working on a difficult case.

"OK, I have to run, Tai. I have to finish a report tonight." It's true but I'm also afraid Tai might want to move in with me for a few months. Tai was not in favor of our separation. He is a very good man—my mother, his mother, our families and our friends have told me this. I agree, too.

I am not as good as Tai. I worked for the boat people early in our marriage but it became too much for me. I need some joy in life. Tai's response to my grievances when we were married was: "Think about boat people. How bad it is for them." I agonized over them for several years but finally I said, "I can't care about the boat people anymore. It's making me too sad and depressed." Tai was stunned by my hardness. I left, moved out of the townhouse in Falls Church and got an apartment in Arlington. I have my own income from my IBM job.

To avoid Tai I go to the Korean supermarket in Merrifield for Vietnamese garden rolls to eat at home. The fruit and vegetables at the Korean supermarket are much better than the chain supermarkets and the shoppers make me feel comfortable. It's crowded with Asian and Latino people. The aisles are narrow and worn down. You have to walk sideways to get around the stacked food and the other customers.

In the produce section large stacks of casaba, yucca and fava beans on barrels block the way. The Asian pears look almost as good as those in the outside market in Hue near the Huong River; we call it the Perfume River because it smells so fragrant. I select a few Asian pears for lunch.

"Linh Hoa, is that you?" a voice next to me says. I turn and recognize a cosmetologist friend I have not seen in a while.

"Sang! How are you?"

Sang is from Hue too but we never met until we came to America. Madame Van at the Hue Academy taught both Sang and I how to walk gracefully in our *Ao Dai* dresses. "Practice. Practice. Practice," she said. "The book will not fall from your head, Linh Hoa, if you cross your hands behind your back and grasp your elbows. This will teach you how to hold your shoulders."

I still think a group of young women in *Ao Dai* is the most graceful sight with the silky colorful tunic split at the sides showing the white flowing trousers underneath. Last April when I wore my bright blue *Ao Dai* with white trousers to commemorate the fall of Saigon at Eden Center I felt very Vietnamese even though I'm a naturalized American citizen.

"You look so pretty, Sang. Vietnamese women are elegant, don't you think?" I say flirtatiously. She meets my eyes and we smile the way Madame Van taught us. I wish I had Sang's beautiful bone structure. I think my face is too fat but Sang says I exaggerate. She has given me good makeup tips to improve my features. I outline my eyes and my lips to show them at their best although my lips are quite full without makeup.

"You look stunning, Linh Hoa. Very few people dress so stylishly for work anymore. Are you trying to attract Tai?" I am wearing a brown silk Tahari suit with a cream-colored satin blouse that has a high Asian collar. My clothes are quite expensive but I need all the confidence I can buy

"Tai and I separated, Sang."

"Oh, no!" she says, "I am so sorry to hear that." Her eyes fill with tears.

"It's O.K., Sang. I want the separation," I say laying my hand softly on her arm. I am tired of getting this kind of sympathy and I change the subject.

"Have you seen Minh Hanh lately?" I ask.

"Yes. She is expecting her baby soon," Sang says.

"Oh, how nice, I know she and Ca-Dao want a child."

"Yes. But they are not doing well. Ca-Dao lost his job." Sang says, "Why don't you call her. I'm sure she would like to hear from you."

"I will," I say, but I know I am too depressed to follow through. We say goodbye.

I go over to the prepared food section and get the garden rolls and also grilled beef with lemongrass. I am so exhausted when I get home and I feel so blue I don't eat anything. I go to my room and write a check for $100 to Minh Hanh and put it in an envelope with a note about her expected baby.

Then I draft an engineering test report until midnight. Engineering is a comfort to me. I don't worry about feelings when I'm concentrating on engineering so I spend long hours working. Tai says new Americans have to work hard to prove themselves.

In the morning I take the grilled beef with lemongrass and the Asian pear for lunch but I am so hungry I open the plastic container and start eating the beef in the lab at 10:00 a.m. The spicy smell of lemongrass fills the lab.

"Don't spill that on the power supply," Karen jokes. Karen is my closest Caucasian friend. She is much older than me but is kind and concerned when I tell her about my problems.

Eating in the lab is not allowed but I am always starving, so I eat continually but still weigh only ninety pounds. Karen is the project manager but she says she has bigger fish to fry than policing the lab for rule breakers like me. Karen helps me learn American idioms which I write down in a spiral notebook that I keep next to the dictionary on my desk. When I came to America at fifteen I spoke only Vietnamese but now Karen says I speak English better than most people born here.

At lunch I peel the Asian pear and offer a piece to Karen.

"This pear is so hard. It tastes more like an apple than a pear," she says eating it.

"I think it tastes different than American apples or pears," I say.

"Ah, there it is. You like eating them because they're Asian," Karen teases me.

"No. I honestly like them. In Hue our meals have a sourness and bitterness to them. We don't use sugar and coconut milk very much. But there are a lot of American ways I like better than Asian ways. I think American men are nicer than Asian men."

"Linh Hoa, you want an American man who will eat Asian food seven days a week. I don't think such a person exists."

"There are American men I know who like Asian food very much," I say.

"At best you may find a man who will go 50/50 on Asian and American food," she says

"What about Charlie? He's married to a Korean woman who cooks Asian food," I say.

"Charlie eats hamburgers and French fries for lunch. I've seen him," Karen says.

"Maybe I do want something that doesn't exist. But I want a man who gives me attention and sympathy and I don't know any Vietnamese men who treat their wives like that. Tai doesn't.

My father doesn't. My brothers don't. My cousins don't. And my friends' husbands don't, as far as I can tell."

"You are so conflicted," Karen says, "you know what we do in America when we are so conflicted?'

"What?" I ask

"See a therapist," she says.

"I am seeing a Filipino therapist," I say, "she is very nice to talk to but she has no real answers for me."

*   *   *

The next day my mother calls me at work. We talk in Vietnamese.

"Linh Hoa, I got a call from Mother Trinh An. She said Tai Chinh has no place to stay. He needs a place to sleep for two months."

"Mother, you know I am separated from Tai."

"He is still your husband, Linh Hoa. He is your husband."

"I can't have him stay here, Mother. It would affect the divorce."

"What divorce? Why are you talking divorce now?" She is so angry; I listen and say nothing.

After my mother is through scolding me I call Tai. "Tai, I'm doing this out of honor for my mother who asked. You can sleep on the sofa in my living room until your apartment is ready in December, if you want. But we're still separated and I'm not cooking for you or washing your clothes."

Tai gives his nervous laugh. "A million thanks. Your sofa is much better than my yoga mat."

Karen and I go to Pho 75 for lunch the next day. The customers sit together at long tables and are served beef noodle and chicken noodle soup in oversized china bowls. I reach over and sprinkle basil leaves and bean sprouts over Karen's Pho to show her our customs. "I washed my hands," I assure her. She smiles. She knows how I use many paper towels to wash my hands and leave the restroom without touching the door handle.

"My husband is staying in my apartment for a couple of months," I tell her.

Karen looks perplexed. "Linh Hoa, won't that affect your divorce process?"

"Yes. We may have to wait a year after this," I say, "But I don't care. I'm not planning to get married again—at least not for a while." I smile.

"Are you sure you want to get divorced, Linh Hoa?" Karen asks.

"Yes. I lived with Tai for twelve years and I know what his answer is for every problem in our marriage. 'Think about the boat people.' I don't want to think about bad news anymore. On the day my family left Vietnam we went to the roof of the American Embassy and we left in a helicopter. Bombs were exploding around us."

"Weren't you terrified?" Karen asks.

"I was fifteen. Everything was happening so fast. I remember the excitement. We were told we could bring one suitcase with us. I wore two dresses so I could take an extra dress for my grandmother," I say proudly.

Karen wonders, "Were you one of the boat people?"

"No. The helicopters took us to ships. Our ship was medium sized but so dirty and crowded. Maybe we would be boat people if my mother didn't get us tickets for the helicopter. She worked as a secretary to an American colonel and he got us out."

"I can't imagine suffering through that. No wonder you are so concerned with germs," Karen says.

"But Tai was a boat person. He didn't come here until 1978 and he risked his life in a little boat which had to travel far to

Malaysia. So now he feels he has to do everything he can to help the other boat people."

Karen shakes her head amazed by my story.

* * *

Persimmon season lasts a month towards the end of the year so I am going to the Korean Supermarket to get persimmons while they last. In the produce section I notice a few plantains have fallen onto the floor and shoppers are tripping over them. Several potatoes are on the floor and I wonder when it was last cleaned. I am searching for the best persimmons when a tall Caucasian man says, "Excuse me. You remind me of a woman I knew in Vietnam."

"I don't think so," I say.

"Your name isn't Kim Tran?" he says.

"No. It is Linh Hoa Nguyen," I say.

"I'm sorry. You look like her," he says.

"Was she pretty?" I flirt with him.

"Very," he replies.

"Do you say that to every Vietnamese woman who comes in here?" I smile at him. I am wearing a gold satin Chinese blouse with high collar and a full-length black crepe skirt.

"No. I really thought you were her," he says, "I met her in Hue when I returned for a visit last year. I was in the Vietnam war."

"I come from Hue," I say.

"It's so beautiful there. I'd like to visit there again," he says.

"I would like to visit Hue too, but I can't." I think about the inner courtyard of our house in Hue with the small lotus pond and the miniature bonsai trees Grandfather trimmed so faithfully every day. Also the bamboo passages where we played when we were children.

"Why not?" he asks.

"It would be too dangerous for me. I'm considered a political enemy because of my work with the boat people.

"It's great that you help the boat people," he says.

"Oh, no, it's my husband who did so much for them. I helped him just a little bit." This was not quite true. When Tai brought the boat people home, I would cook for them or clean their clothes, teach them English, or try to find them a sponsor or place to live or listen to their desperate stories. But how many desperate stories can one person hear without getting desperate herself?

The Caucasian man looks dejected when I mentioned Tai. "We are separated now," I say. I did not tell him we are separated only by the hallway between the living room and the bedroom.

"Here's my card if you want to have coffee sometime to talk about Hue or anything else," he says.

"Thank you," I say giving my charming Hue smile. Karen says I'm naïve but I know when to pull out of a dangerous situation. I did survive the fall of Saigon.

I look at the card and read John Trotter, Systems Analyst, Price Waterhouse. He is in the same kind of field, so we have more in common than Hue. He is what I search for at the Korean supermarket besides the persimmons and Asian pears. Maybe I will call him.

In the prepared food section I buy some sour fish soup and pork and shrimp summer rolls for Tai.

I'm hungry when I get home so I eat dinner with Tai but afterwards go into my bedroom and document a lab test report until midnight.

At lunch the next day I slice the persimmons for Karen who has never tasted one. They are an Asian delicacy. It's two o'clock and the cafeteria is almost empty. I tell her about John Trotter.

"You have mixed emotions, Linh Hoa," Karen says, "You

flirt with a Vietnam vet stranger who cases the Korean super-market and then feed your ex who you have sleeping in your living room."

"I know. I'm hopeless," I say, "I don't know what I'm look-ing for. Whatever I left in Hue, I guess."

One morning when the sun was beginning to rise in Hue, my mother said, "Wakeup, Linh Hoa. We must hurry. Enemy is coming." I did not even say goodbye to Dieu-Kiem, my best friend, who later drowned with the boat people. I did not say goodbye to all the places we rode our bicycles: along the banks of the Perfume River where women with their Vietnamese tra-ditional conical hats rode in sampans on the river singing folk songs we learned in school or along streets next to Hue's gar-dens and courtyards blossoming with jasmine flowers and ly-chee trees, orchids and climbing roses, bamboo trees and pome-granates, pineapple and persimmon trees.

* * *

In the evening I stop at the Little Viet carry-out restaurant in Eden Center for grilled chicken sandwiches for dinner for Tai and me. I admire the sound of the high-pitched tones of Vietnamese as a young girl at the cash register talks to an older woman. She reminds me of Dieu-Kiem whom I thought about earlier in the afternoon. I don't notice Tai's mother is in the line behind me until it is too late to leave. I go over and kiss Mother Trinh An and we talk for a few minutes about relatives. Then she barks, "You and Tai should live together for good. He needs a good wife's support. He is so important for Vietnamese Americans. You know that."

"I know. Tai is doing such good work. He is a wonderful man. But I cannot be married to a saint," I say.

"What kind talk," she says angrily and turns away to leave with her food. I go home dejected.

"Did I do something?" Tai asks.

"No. I have a headache." I take my sandwich into my bleak bedroom and eat it there.

I decide to call John Trotter. He suggests we go to lunch but I ask if he would take me to the Kings Dominion amusement park. Tai would never go to such a place. He said he is not a child. John agrees to the amusement park even though he tells me he can't go on the rides. He suffers from vertigo ever since he was wounded in Vietnam.

Waiting for the ride to start, I see John down below watching me. He is holding a large orange tiger he won for me at the shooting arcade. I like men to admire me and I feel pretty today. I am wearing a see-through white nylon blouse with a black lacy bra from Victoria Secret. But I have no intention of getting intimate with John. I am still a married woman. I want to have a little fun and pretend for one evening I am happy and belong with someone.

"You looked dreamy up there, Linh Hoa," John says, "With your eyes closed and your head tilted toward the sky you seemed to be in another world."

"I am, John. I am in Hue," I say.

"Maybe someday we can both return to Hue together," he says. I hold onto his muscular arm and smile at him. I am attracted to his large physique next to my small body. He seems so much more manly and protective than Tai.

I offer John the garden rolls I brought for our snack but instead he buys hotdogs and French fries for us to eat. American food makes me sick so John has to finish my hotdog. He watches me ride on five or six amusement park attractions and then takes me home. Since Tai is in my apartment, I say goodbye to John outside. I think he is disappointed I don't ask him inside. It was a nice date but I can see he is too American for me.

As I am opening my door, I hear a man talking in Vietnamese.

My apartment is very humble and furnished only with a sectional sofa in the living room and a coffee table. I have not really settled in.

I am troubled when I see Tai in the living room talking to another Vietnamese man. There are three Vietnamese children huddled against the wall and a Vietnamese woman hugging one of the little girls.

"I told Chinh he could stay here for a few days with his family until we find them a place to live," Tai says speaking in English and pointing to the Vietnamese man.

"But Tai there is no room here for five more people," I say.

"There is more room here than on boat they escape from Vietnam," he shouts. He bullies me by standing close and yelling so I can't refuse.

"O.K., Tai. They can sleep on the floor," I say.

"Could you get blankets for them?" he asks humbly.

"I don't have many blankets," I say, but he gets angry with me again. "Old coats then or towels," he barks.

I search through the whole house for clothes or coats or blankets for the boat people. "We are grateful," he says but then adds in Vietnamese, "And could little Le Mai sleep in your bed with you? She is trembling and needs rest." Her mother smiles at Tai for making this request. "O.K.," I say. I am defeated.

I go into my bedroom with Le Mai. "Don't be afraid. You will be alright now." I stroke her hair but realize she needs a bath so I go into the bathroom and fill the bathtub with warm water. I take her into the bathroom and wash her hair and everything else until she smells like Dial soap. I find an old T-shirt for her to sleep in and then tuck her into bed kissing her forehead. How many times I did this in the past I cannot count.

I use my computer and then crawl into bed myself. I turn my back to Le Mai in the bed and silently sob. I don't belong with these people and I don't belong with John either.

The next day I call into work sick. I go to a job search company to look for a position in another city to get out of Northern Virginia.

"Where do you want to work?" the job search assistant asks. I am surprised by the question but quickly calculate the farthest distance from Virginia.

"California," I say.

"Where in California?" she asks.

"Any place," I answer.

"It's a big state," she seems perplexed.

"I think a few minutes and say, "Los Angeles"

It takes two weeks for the job search company to find me a job. Hardware test engineers are in high demand in 1995. Tai, his family, my family, Karen and everyone else I know implores me not to go but I pack quickly and leave. I resettle in Orange County in early January.

* * *

"The persimmon tree needs water, Pham" I say to my fiancé. We are working in the garden of our Mission-style house in Orange County. I met Pham at the office shortly after moving to California a year ago. He is five years younger than me and came to America when he was a child. He is very American but still eats my Vietnamese dinners.

"I hear that in my sleep now," he says. Pham planted the persimmon tree in our yard on the day we moved in. "It will give us the roots we are looking for," he said. Each week Pham plants another flower or bush in our yard. We have white hibiscus, pink impatiens with double blossoms like little roses, lavender butterfly bushes and periwinkle orchids. The entire backyard has become a garden needing our continual attention. We water the persimmon tree and our plants for twenty minutes before we go to work and then spend an hour in the evening weeding or planting another flower. It is tiring after a long day of engineering but we work at it together and are pleased with our results.

I don't think about Hue as much now. But I sometimes think I might like to move to Toronto where there is a large population of Vietnamese from Hue and sometimes I wonder if I would feel more at home in Seattle which also has a large Vietnamese community.

Pham has finished watering the plants and says, "Let's eat our lemongrass chicken on the terrace this evening. I'll turn the garden lanterns on and we can admire our work." He is so young and full of life he makes me forget my restless thoughts. I hope he is right about the roots of the persimmon tree.

Marvelous

I read the handwritten greeting card from Mr. Anthony, my hairstylist of twelve years and sighed. It was an announcement he was leaving Chez Michel's. I was upset at the thought of searching for a new hairdresser. Occasionally when Mr. Anthony was unavailable and I had to accept a substitute at Chez Michel's, I experienced a number of disappointing haircuts. Mr. Anthony suggested in his card he would be willing to cut hair in his home for his loyal clients but I didn't like the intimacy implied. I considered my relationship with my hair stylist to begin and end at the doorway of the hair salon.

"Would love to see you, but if I don't, thank you for your marvelous friendship," he wrote. I sensed a need in his note and knew I ultimately would call for an appointment. But the prospect of navigating through an unfamiliar Washington D.C. neighborhood in search of an unknown townhouse to get my hair trimmed annoyed me. I was shy and had trouble with entrances.

Two weeks later on a crisp October Saturday afternoon, I parked my car in a spot vacated by a BMW near Mr. Anthony's address. The gleaming sun fell against the row of townhouses on the deserted block of U Street northeast of Dupont Circle casting shadows in cool geometric patterns evoking the loneliness of an Edward Hopper painting. Since I was five minutes late for my appointment, I hurried down the solitary block looking at each townhouse number until I found Mr. Anthony's address at the end of the street.

The entranceway to his house was sunken and I walked hesitantly down the three steps. Ringing the doorbell, I stood self-consciously in front of the door irritated to be idling in front of this strange townhouse. I clutched the wrought iron grill protecting the door and peered into the small, translucent window. Unable to distinguish anything within, I attempted to use the metal doorknocker but an evergreen wreath rendered it useless.

He must have forgotten about my appointment, I thought. I banged against the hardwood door stinging the knuckles of my hand. Was I at the correct address? Except for a bowl of milk on the brick ledge flanking the entrance, there was no sign of life. I examined the card, concerned a stranger might appear from behind the door. It was the correct address but I was ready to leave. Muffled sounds from the other side of the door raised my hopes. The door burst open and Mr. Anthony stood on the threshold, ablaze with cheer.

"Come in. Come in. Oh, it's so marvelous to see you again," he gushed.

"Hello. I was hoping I was at the right house," I said pausing a moment before entering his home. Mr. Anthony was dressed in a white T-shirt with cut off sleeves and white shorts resembling boxer underwear giving me qualms. He looked pale and woefully thin.

"Did you knock? I didn't hear you. I said to Pauline, 'She's not coming.' But then I went to look and there you were. Pauline! Pauline!" Mr. Anthony was as animated as ever.

Pauline, Mr. Anthony's wife, entered the room dressed in a full-length crimson and gold robe. Mr. Anthony regaled me with stories of their theatergoing at the salon. I could never reconcile Mr. Anthony being married since he appeared to be gay.

Now the mystery deepened since Pauline seemed to be a generation older than Mr. Anthony who was about fifty.

"Pauline, I want you to meet my client, Clare. Oh, isn't this marvelous. I'm so glad you came." Mr. Anthony ushered me into a small dimly-lit kitchen. The sun, which entered through an elevated basement window above the sink, provided one bright patch of light on the opposite wall. The kitchen was tastefully designed with solid oak cabinets lining two walls. The hardwood floor was flawless and beautifully waxed and most of the kitchen appliances had a smoky grey glass façade. Near the kitchen door stood a small circular table of black wrought iron and translucent glass. Two matching chairs with rounded ice cream parlor seats were at the table.

"This is my salon, Madame," Mr. Anthony said accenting the second syllable. "Please sit down," he said laughing at his pretentiousness. I balanced myself cautiously on one of the ice cream parlor chairs.

"Would you like coffee?" he asked.

"No, thank you," I said responding the same way I had each time he asked for the last twelve years.

"Tea?"

"No, thanks." I never drank anything at the hair salon.

"I was telling Pauline. This is the woman who's been to Venice and loves it like us. She's the one who told me about Visconti's *Death in Venice*," Mr. Anthony continued.

I did like Venice but not like Mr. Anthony who watched *Death in Venice*, starring Dirk Bogarde, once a month ever since I mentioned it. It was the Thomas Mann story of an aging gentleman scholar who has a covert flirtation with a beautiful youth, like Michelangelo's David, who he observes at Venice's Lido beach. Rather than leave Venice and his obsessive passion when a plague breaks out, he stays and ultimately succumbs to the disease.

Mr. Anthony and I shared intellectual interests in books,

movies, Europe and the arts. I didn't realize this until three years after we met. The first time I visited Chez Michel's, I felt outclassed in the salon which catered to the social elite of Washington. As usual I had trouble finding the entrances: to the salon, to the correct floor, to the dressing room and to Mr. Anthony's station. But Mr. Anthony, who was short and a few pounds overweight, overlooked my awkwardness and treated me as though I was a longtime customer. I felt indebted to him for helping me overcome my inertia and make changes in my life starting with a dramatically different hair style.

I usually kept our conversations to questions of haircare but then one day I saw an old hard-covered book at Mr. Anthony's station and ventured, "I see you are reading *Anna Karenina*."

"What? Oh, yes. It's marvelous. I can't put it down. This is the fourth time I've read it and it's even better," he responded. Each appointment thereafter Mr. Anthony and I discussed books, movies, television specials, operas, and ballets. I began looking forward to getting my haircut and even prepared for it by viewing a few foreign "art" films.

Combing my hair into sections he said, "And remember *Don't Look Now* with Donald Sutherland." He had searched out every movie filmed in Venice. "How beautiful the canals were. Even the marvelous funeral cortege at the end with the three women in their black dresses standing at the helm of the lead boat. Marvelous. Even funerals look romantic in Venice," he laughed. He was in a reverie but I felt a pang as I recalled the recent death of my father with my three sisters dressed in black at the gravesite. I was still mourning a parent.

Pauline brought a tray containing several varieties of teas and placed it on the glass table where I sat.

I looked at her perplexed.

"She didn't want any. Did you? Or did you? Mr. Anthony said nervously.

"I'm sorry. I never drink caffeine."

Apparently Pauline was hard of hearing. She took the tray away, showing no emotion, like a waiter in an elegant restaurant.

Mr. Anthony prepared to cut my hair by parting it into sections. I noticed he was grasping my hair firmly before cutting it to steady his hand.

"So why did you leave Chez Michel's?" I asked.

"Oh, I've been disgusted with them for a while, Madame. They wanted me to push their products on my clients. I'm very sorry, Madame, but I am not a salesman; I'm a hair stylist." Mr. Anthony sounded as if he was trying to convince himself as well as me. His hands were shaking and I was glad he was deliberating over each lock of hair he clipped.

Several times over twelve years of haircuts, I considered leaving him and finding a new hairdresser. There was the time he broke his finger and it was in a splint. During his recovery period, my haircuts were less than satisfying. But I decided a few chopped haircuts were worth the many outstanding haircuts plus the mutual respect between us.

Shortly after I met him, he went on a diet and lost so much weight I thought he might be seriously ill. He started wearing white tapered Italian shirts open to his chest displaying a collection of antique gold chains. He was so thin and gaunt a figure, I suspected he had an eating disorder.

As he moved from my right side to cut the other side of my hair, I observed he looked anorexic.

"I told Pauline I was so anxious to see you. I've been looking forward to Saturday all week," Mr. Anthony said. Pauline sat on the wrought iron chair next to the refrigerator and seemed pleased my presence was making Mr. Anthony happy. She did not appear to understand everything being said, contributing a few muted comments. I glanced toward her trying to discern her age. She was turned toward Mr. Anthony who nodded in her direction from time to time but never acknowledged the disparity in their ages in any way.

"I woke this morning and said to Pauline, 'She's coming today. You have to meet her. She loves Venice as much as we do.' You know, Pauline and I spent two months in Venice shortly after we married. We stayed with a friend at his marvelous villa overlooking the Piazza San Marco. Pauline taught both of us ballet but he became the *premier danseur* for the Venice Opera and I became a hair stylist." Mr. Anthony's exhilaration ended with feigned sobbing.

"I was watching a tape of Lawrence Olivier in *Brideshead Revisited* last night," he said resuming his enthusiasm. "He is the greatest actor. And the scenery in Venice. Marvelous."

"You know, I recorded the thirteen episodes of *Brideshead* when it was on Public Broadcasting," I said. "I love that series. It's one of the few films I can watch over and over. Also *Passage to India* and Peter Weir's movies like *Witness*."

"Oh, *Witness*. What a movie. The photography is so marvelous. And what did he have to work with? Pennsylvania corn fields and the stark Amish farms. Yet the angles and the designs are so marvelously filmed. It's pretty bad if you can't make a beautiful film out of the Himalayas like in *Passage to India* but the artistry of *Witness* was made out of nothing—an old barn on a dismal day in a cow pasture."

I was going to discuss a book I read by Toni Morrison but Mr. Anthony was steeped in the classics rather than in modern literature. Antiquated hard-covered books like *Madame Bovary*, *David Copperfield* and *War and Peace*, which he claimed to have read eleven times, lay on his makeup table amid the latest copies of *Vogue* and *Glamour*.

Intent on giving me the perfect haircut, he clipped my hair very deliberately, perhaps to ensure my return. I sensed an undercurrent of desperation in his actions. As he grasped my hair,

I felt his need to cling to something real. Although he was as effervescent as ever, there was an elusive sadness beneath the surface as if he were questioning his role in life.

"Mr. Robert said you were going into the computer field," I said raising the sensitive subject of Mr. Anthony's unemployed status.

"Oh, I tried that but it wasn't what I thought it would be," he said dejectedly. "It was keying the information in. One of my clients suggested it. And I thought it would be different. But it was nothing. I'm sure I would become very bored, Madame."

I worked for years as a project manager for a computer firm and could think of no one more ill-suited for the computer field than Mr. Anthony but I said, "Well, at least, you gave it a try and found out it wasn't for you."

"Yes. It was incredibly different. I'm going to take my time and look around for a while before I go back to work. Francois wants me to cut hair for him. I could go there any time. But I told Pauline I probably wouldn't have this opportunity again. So I'm taking advantage of the time off to relax and take things easy. The other day I walked two miles to Key Bridge to take pictures of the swollen river level. The water was two yards below the bridge. I could almost reach down to touch it. It was marvelous. I was so excited. Wasn't I, Pauline?"

Pauline shook her head in agreement mumbling unintelligibly.

I began to suspect Mr. Anthony was going through a midlife crisis. At fifty-two he was assessing whether the life of a hair-stylist was defensible. He had a number of peripheral relation-ships with his clients, but was that enough? I considered him a casual acquaintance I saw once every six or seven weeks for an hour or less.

"And what are you doing, Madame? Did you change your position yet?" he asked.

"Yes, I start in two weeks at my new job with a telecommunications company," I said. "It's a whole new career change."

"Oh, marvelous. I'm so excited for you," he said exuberantly. "And how long did you work at your old position?"

"Almost twenty years," I answered. I had just celebrated my fortieth birthday and my life was on an upswing. Besides beginning a new career, I was taking a painting course at the Corcoran Art Gallery which I always wanted to do.

"Twenty years. Incredible. I wish you luck, Madame. It's good to make a change. I guess we're both at the same crossroads," Mr. Anthony laughed thoroughly amused. He brushed the cut hairs from my neck as he finished my haircut.

"There, Madame. I think you will feel a good bit lighter now with your beautiful head of hair thinned out. Oh, it's so nice seeing you. Would you like the grand tour?" he said.

"That would be nice," I said haltingly. Although my inclination was to leave, I didn't want to refuse his offer. Mr. Anthony led me into the adjacent dining room overwhelmed by a jungle of greenery. A mission-style dining table of heavy, rough wood stood in one corner of the room and appeared unused with no apparent path to access it. The dining room led to a modest patio also decorated with a profusion of plants. A young maple tree threatened to dwarf the miniature backyard and the patio one day.

"I stole the maple tree from Rock Creek Park when it was a few feet tall. Pauline couldn't believe I brought it home on the Metro," he laughed. He started up the narrow staircase and guided me to the second level of the house. Pauline trailed behind. The half-tones of the late afternoon darkened the second floor living room. A large glass exhibit case containing a collection of Asian figurines obstructed the entrance to the living room. I squeezed by the fragile display enthralled by the colorful jade, alabaster, and soapstone miniature Asian ladies.

"This is Pauline's. She's been collecting these Asian ladies for years especially when we visit Venice or Paris. They are all the rage in the grand stores along the Rue del la Paix in Paris. Pauline can't get enough of them.

Christmas tree lights adorned two six-foot potted plants in the living room. "We decorated these at Christmas time and I thought they looked so marvelous I convinced Pauline to leave them up this year," Mr. Anthony laughed. His exuberance masked his earlier undertone of despair.

"And what do you think about my Ann Packard painting, Madame?" he said admiring a medium-sized painting of the Cape Cod seashore. "I went to a small gallery at lunch one day and I saw this painting for sale. I fell instantly in love with it. It reminded me of the Adriatic. And when I found out it was a genuine Ann Packard I decided I had to buy it immediately so I rushed to my bank to take out a loan. The banker was incredulous when I told him I needed $3000 to buy a painting." Mr. Anthony was enjoying this recollection immensely as he laughed excessively. "But I am very happy with it, Madame, very happy."

"And look at this," he said stooping down to lift a massive granite sculpture of several gods and goddesses from India. Pauline's uncle gave this to us. I admired it so much he was forced to give it to us." Mr. Anthony roared through his description of the events. "There was nothing else he could do but give it to me. I know he was a bit annoyed but I kept saying, 'Isn't it marvelous? Marvelous.' He finally gave it to me to shut me up," Mr. Anthony lunged over with laughter.

He continued the tour to the top floor of the townhouse. We entered a small den housing his beloved classics. Bookcases lined three of the four walls. The books were hard covered. They were not leather-bound or purchased from a Great Books mail order company but rather musty old books—the kind you find in a small town library or an antique store.

On the remaining wall there was a decorative curio shelf completely filled with one-inch ceramic replicas of cats. "This is Pauline's collection of cats," Mr. Anthony smiled. "I have to show you Buffy in the bedroom." He began laughing hysterically. As we entered the master bedroom, Mr. Anthony headed toward a shelf at the top of the bed. Still roaring, he retrieved a small artistically-engraved wooden box, wrapped around with a ribbon. "This is Puffy, my cat. She died and I didn't have the heart to bury her. So I had her ashes placed in this box. Poor Puffy." His laughter had a hint of genuine sympathy. The image of my recently deceased father came to mind. After they buried him in the ground, I thought what a terrible thing to do to him. Perhaps, he would be better off in an attractive box like Puffy.

Mr. Anthony pointed out the guest bedroom and then slowly walked me down to the entrance level of the townhouse. When we came to the foyer, he seemed reluctant to say goodbye and we talked about art a few minutes more.

"I've also been painting reproductions of the impressionists to develop a better understanding of color," I said.

"Oh, marvelous," he gushed. But then it was time for me to leave and we said goodbye.

"Oh, hair, grow fast so she'll come again," he said gleefully. But his gaiety was tinged with sadness and his desperation was obvious.

As I left the darkened house, I was greeted by the intensity of the sun on the horizon as it was beginning to set. Mr. Anthony walked me to the corner in the crisp October afternoon even though he was clad only in his white shorts and shirt. He pointed out his route to Chez Michel's and the neighborhood attractions before his final goodbye.

After we parted, he shouted to me, "Bring your paintings next time. Bring your paintings."

I debated with myself about whether I would return for

further haircuts, but throughout the winter and spring I went to Mr. Anthony's kitchen to have my hair trimmed. Once I even brought along four small impressionistic imitations and there were more "Marvelouses" than I could count. Even though I recognized his gushing as supportiveness, he did help affirm my part-time life as a painter.

In the spring I was notified in the mail by Pauline that Mr. Anthony was unable to work anymore due to a serious liver ailment. And it was only a few months later that she sent me a note informing me Mr. Anthony had died of liver cancer.

During the year following Mr. Anthony's death I wandered from hairdresser to hairdresser trying to revive my haircut. After each haircut I would look in the mirror with disappointment and regret.

As I opened the door to leave Chez Michel's, espying my latest chopped-off haircut in the store's plate-glass windows, I felt like the ancient Greek mourners who chopped off their hair or slashed their clothes in protest of a death. My thoughts were on Mr. Anthony. I stepped into the hypnotic cadence of the rain and envisioned him dying as he watched his favorite movie, *Death in Venice*. A year after his death I was still grieving for a person I knew casually but who had greater impact on me than I had thought, his death coming two years after the death of my father. I was accumulating losses and I could expect others. A smell, a look, an image, a place recalled the loss when least expected.

My thoughts returned to *Death in Venice*. I could see the camera pan to the Adriatic and to the Grand Canal accompanied by a melancholy adagio. I could see the Santa Maria della Salute rising majestically from the sea. I could hear Mr. Anthony whisper gently as he died—"Marvelous."

ANDREA VOJTKO

A ndrea Vojtko is a writer and artist residing in Arlington, Virginia. She was nominated in 2003 for a Pushcart Prize for her short story, "Jubilant Voices." Her fiction has appeared in the Anthology *Puzzles of Faith and Patterns of Doubt*, the Anthology *Being Human: Call of the Wild*, the *Potomac Review*, *Words of Wisdom* and *Road and Travel*. She is a member of The Writer's Center in Bethesda, Maryland where she took part in many fiction writing workshops. She received a B.S. degree in mathematics from Misericordia University in Dallas, Pennsylvania and an M.A. degree in mathematics from George Washington University in Washington, D.C. She worked for many years as a Project Manager of Computer and Data Communications projects both in the Federal government and Sprint. Besides writing short stories, she is an avid naturalist, painter and genealogist.

NOTES ON STORIES

1. "Swirling Above Her Head" and "The All-Knowing Eye" both appeared in the anthology, *Being Human: Call of the Wild*, edited by Gregory F. Tague, Editions Bibliotekos, Inc., Fredericka A. Jacks, Publisher, 2012.
2. "Chasing the Loon" appeared in the literary magazine, *Potomac Review: A Journal of Arts and Humanities*, published by Montgomery College, edited by Christa Watters, Issue 40, 2005.
3. "Searching for Life on Mars" appeared in the anthology, *Puzzles of Faith and Patterns of Doubt*, edited by Gregory F. Tague, Editions Bibliotekos, Inc. Fredericka A. Jacks, Publisher, 2013.
4. "Jubilant Voices" appeared in the literary magazine, *Words of Wisdom*, edited by Mikhammad Bin Muhandis Abdel-Ishara, Publisher, J. M. Freiermuth, Volume 22, No. 3, September 2003. "Jubilant Voices" was nominated for a 2003 Pushcart Prize.
5. The above five stories have been re-edited for this publication. The remaining stories in this collection have not been previously published.